I0524778

# THE
# BEACON

*Book 3 in The Muladach Series*

## MELISSA PLANTZ

**FIRE and GRACE**
Publishing, LLC

Copyright © 2021
Melissa Plantz
FIRE and GRACE Publishing, LLC
THE BEACON
*Book 3 in The Muladach Series*
All rights reserved.

No part of this publication may be reproduced, distributed, or transmitted in any form or by any means, including photocopying, recording, or other electronic or mechanical methods, without the prior written permission of the publisher, except in the case of brief quotations embodied in critical reviews and certain other non-commercial uses permitted by copyright law.

Melissa Plantz
FIRE and GRACE Publishing, LLC
fireandgracepublishing.com

Printed in the United States of America
First Printing 2021
First Edition 2021

ISBN: ISBN 978-1-7354248-1-1

10 9 8 7 6 5 4 3 2 1

Unless otherwise indicated, all Scripture quotations are taken from the *Holy Bible*, New Living Translation, copyright 1996, 2004, 2015 by Tyndale House Foundation. Used by permission of Tyndale House Publishers, Carol Stream, Illinois 60188. All rights reserved.

This book is a work of fiction. Names, characters, places, and incidents are the products of the author's imagination or are used fictitiously. Any resemblance to actual events, locales, or persons, living or dead, is entirely coincidental.

Cover Design by VC Book Cover Design

For the **real** Ainsleys and Alecs of the world.

*"You are a light of the world – like a city on a hilltop that cannot be hidden." (Matthew 5:14)*

*"So let's not get tired of doing what is good. At just the right time we will reap a harvest of blessing if we don't give up." (Galatians 6:9)*

# CHAPTER ONE

"Good job, Ainsley," Stephen Reeves said as I picked up my gun and slid a new clip in before switching on the safety and holstering it. The pastor watched me as I pulled my black leather jacket on, carefully concealing the weapon.

"Are you headed back to North Carolina tonight?" he asked.

"Yeah, I have midterms to finish up. As it stands now, I won't get any sleep before my next exam."

He patted me on the shoulder. "I know. I'm sorry. I wouldn't have called you if it wasn't urgent."

I smiled up at the dark-haired man with the tattoos and laid-back attitude. "That's why I came. Don't feel bad about that. How's the little boy?"

"He'll be fine now. The authorities will get him back to his parents."

I nodded. The demons, what we referred to as Muladach now, had led me to a ring of sex traffickers. Thank God, with Stephen's help, we'd found not only the two men kidnapping children, but I'd tracked the demons to the ring itself. Hopefully, these men would go to prison for a long time.

"Have you talked to Kyle lately?" Stephen asked.

"Just through text. He's working on his show in L.A., so I don't think he will be back around this way for a while." Kyle Drekr was the television host of a popular paranormal investigative show. The crew went all over the world, seeking out the unknown. Kyle had worked with my father a long time ago and knew without a doubt that demons and ghosts were real, and although he had *not* confirmed my suspicion, I believed his staff integrated a lot of the spooky things seen and heard on the show during post-production. I had no proof, but there was no way Kyle gathered evidence at every location. Plus, he made it a practice to ignore the dead as much as possible now.

With that being said, Kyle was still a powerful Protector, a sort-of guardian for the Seers.

I looked up at Stephen, the preacher from a small church in Charleston, West Virginia, who also worked with the organization Malus Navis expelling demons. Stephen always seemed laid back with his hard-part black hair and stubbled beard, blue eyes, and distressed jeans. I'd always liked him, but I had come to love him now that he and my mom were officially engaged.

"Have you heard from Alec?"

"Alec? Alec Graham?" I asked. Stephen raised an eyebrow. We knew only one Alec.

"Of course not. Alec cut me out of his life four years ago and hasn't looked back. My friend Bronwyn said she saw him once at the Locklyn Gym right before closing. She'd forgotten her purse and ran back in, and he was there working out. The owner, Henry, lets him work out after closing, so he doesn't have to run into other people."

"That's a lot of judging all at once, you think?" Stephen finished loading his gun case, locked it, and stood.

"I'm not judging him," I offered as I took a step back. "He made his decision. If he wanted to stay friends, he wouldn't have just left."

"Didn't *you* tell him to leave?"

"Yeah, maybe." I looked down at the ground for a moment. When Stephen didn't say anything else, I peered back up at him. "Why the sudden interest in my talking to Alec?"

It was Stephen's turn to appear uneasy. He dropped eye contact with me as he shrugged his shoulders. "No reason. He crossed my mind today."

"Then maybe you should pray for him," I quipped and then instantly regretted it. It was true that whenever someone crossed my mind out of the blue, eventually, I would hear something about them; an illness, a tragedy, or even death. When that happens, Stephen had told me always to stop and pray as it was God's way of bringing them to my attention. I certainly didn't want anything bad to happen to Alec.

"Yeah, well, maybe we should pray for him," Stephen said as he started towards the warehouse door. "Come on, let's get you back on the road for that exam."

~ ~ ~

I sat in the uncomfortable metal chair at the DMV with my registration card in my hand. It was time to renew my little Chevy Cruze, and I had procrastinated for too long, so instead of enjoying the perks of the online service, I got to enjoy the crowded DMV this morning. I'd known it was going to be a long morning when I noticed the broken kiosk.

I could so go for a cup of coffee right now, but that would require me to forfeit my number. There was no way I was going to leave after waiting forty minutes.

"Now serving 34-B at Window Number 12," the electronic voice announced.

I practically danced over to Window Number 12 and smiled at the short woman behind the counter wearing the Sophia nametag.

"Can I help you?" she asked in the most monotone of voices.

"I need to renew my registration, please," I answered.

I watched as she studied my paperwork and then typed something into the computer. I crossed my legs. I shouldn't have worn a short knit dress today. Why was it so cold in here? My dress only appeared warm, but my legs were freezing between my black ankle boots and the black material. I should've worn leggings. For the last four years, I'd come to love working out. Weights, Pilates, yoga, spin - I did it all. I took every class at the Locklyn Gym that the owner Henry's wife taught. Kickboxing was my favorite because it had resulted in powerful and defined legs, which I probably showed off a little too much now.

"That will be $54.30 if you are renewing for one year."

I slid my debit card into the machine and waited. "So, are you ready for Christmas?"

Sophia stopped and looked at me like I'd grown a third eye. "Why?"

"What?"

"Why do you want to know?" she asked as she narrowed her eyes.

"Just making conversation," I answered honestly.

The woman made an actual hmph sound and ordered me to withdraw my card. She handed me the receipt and new sticker. "Have a nice day," she said, sounding like a robot.

I fought the urge to roll my eyes and instead answered loudly, "You too! Have a *fabulous* Christmas!" Then I turned on my heel to see someone standing in front of Window Number 14 staring at me. That was okay. I was sure everyone in the DMV was staring at me at this point. He could join the club. I didn't mind being the center of attention anymore.

It wasn't until I went to deliver the man a triumphant smile as I walked past that it registered with me who the man at Window Number 14 was and why he would stare so intently at me.

I walked a little faster out of the DMV building, fighting to breathe. There was no way I would fall apart out in public. As I hurried to my car in the parking lot, I heard him calling my name.

*Girl, just get in the car.* My mind yelled at my fingers to hit the unlock button on my keychain. However, my body, as if having control of itself independently from the rest of me, slowed down and stopped at the driver's side door.

I felt his presence before I smelled his cologne. How could he stand so close after he'd walked away from me four years ago? I raised my gaze to meet Alec Graham's green eyes. He still had the stubble on his face, and his haircut was a little closer to his scalp instead of the messy look he used to wear. He wore a black jacket that looked like it was tailor-made for him. Bronwyn said he was working out after the gym closed, and she wasn't wrong. Even covered by his jacket, I could see that his arms were more prominent, his chest broader.

I had to remind myself to breathe. I wasn't in high school anymore, and I was pretty sure I'd gotten over Alec. At that thought, the voice in my head laughed hysterically.

"Ainsley, I'd hoped it was you," he said. My, how I'd missed his voice.

"It's me," I said weakly and then caught myself. I stood up a little straighter. "I need to go. I have someplace to be," I lied as I threw my long blonde hair over my shoulder.

"Of course. Well, it was good seeing you again. You look…" Alec trailed off as I opened my car door and forced my body to obey me as I sat down, knowing my dress was hiking up a bit further than appropriate. I placed my hand on the inside of the door and looked up at Alec with every bit of coolness I could muster as if waiting for him to finish his sentence.

"You look beautiful," he finally said.

"Oh? Thank you. I thought you were going to say grown-up. Maybe I'll see you around."

The smile on his gorgeous face deflated a bit. I'd hit a nerve. He nodded and took a step back. "Goodbye, Ainsley."

I smiled as I shut my door and started the engine. As I drove back to my dorm, I never really saw the road. All I could see was Alec.

~ ~ ~

"Hey, Reynolds! Stephen told me about you saving that boy from those traffickers. Great job!" Kyle Drekr bellowed into the phone.

"Thanks, but that was all God. I had no clue that's what we would expose." Kyle and I had gone on a few adventures together with the organization, and we still rode each other a bit, but we got along now.

"Are you staying with your mom for Christmas?"

"Yep. I'm going to try to spend some time with Ben." My little brother Benjamin was now a teenager and stood as tall as me at five-foot-six. "Between classes and work, I feel I've neglected him terribly."

"Well, let me know if you want to come out to California. I'm on hiatus from my show until spring."

"I might do that. I've only been there a few times." I remembered the investigation Kyle and I had performed outside of Los Angeles in some caves where a small cluster of demons hid near a portal. It was a beautiful area, but I hadn't had time to explore.

"You're more than welcome to stay. I have an extra bedroom."

"Thanks. I'll let you know. How's Maria?"

"Oh, we broke up. You know how it is. She wanted me to spend more time with her, but between the show, the shoots, and the investigations, I barely have any time for anyone else in my life. How about you?"

"What about me?"

"Are you seeing anyone?"

Telling Kyle about seeing Alec today was on the tip of my tongue. The men hadn't liked each other, and at one point in South Carolina, they'd come to blows over a misunderstanding. Technically, I'd *seen* Alec, but I wasn't *seeing* Alec.

"No. No one right now."

"Well, if you change your mind about California for the holidays, just call."

"I will, I promise." I glanced around my dorm room. As much as I would love to hang out in Los Angeles, I felt Mom and Ben needed me home.

After I ended my call with Kyle, I texted my best friend Molly to call me later. Now she, I could tell all about seeing Alec for the first time in four years. We'd been friends since grade school and were closer than sisters. We'd been through a great deal a few years ago when we got too close to a serial killer influenced by demons, and, unfortunately, Molly had been stabbed and hovered in a coma for more than a week before she woke up. Even then, recovery was long.

I started packing my bags to go home to Locklyn. Thank goodness that since I planned to return for Spring semester, the school allowed me to keep my other items in my single dorm room. When I'd first arrived on campus as a Freshman, the Financial Aid Office explained to me that I would have a double room and that my father's GI bill covered quite a bit of my financial debt. However, I would still need to pay more. I'd been heartbroken. I thought I would have to drop out because there was no way I was about to let Mom take money out of savings while she kept up with the house and utility bills.

But, right after I moved into the double room with a girl I suspected was part demon by choice, I got a call from the Financial Aid office. They couldn't explain how or why, but someone had paid my outstanding balances. Not only that but I was registered for a single room with its own bathroom. *For all four years.* I made the woman check three times and then print me out a receipt showing this information just in case. I'd been able to keep the same room, and it almost seemed like home.

I hated to admit it, but part of me believed that maybe Alec was involved in my debt cancellation. While investigating a mansion in South Carolina, just minutes from Alec's childhood home, I'd learned that Alec came from a very wealthy family. He'd *chosen* police work over a luxury lifestyle.

But then again, it didn't make any sense. Why would the man pay for my schooling not covered by the GI bill for four years and then not so much as bother to call me? I stuffed my sweaters in my bag harder than necessary. I could've asked him. At the DMV, instead of getting in my car with my fake stuck-up attitude, I could've just asked Alec if he had paid the school.

And then what? What if he had said yes? I would feel obligated to pay him back. If he denied it, then I would have to admit to Alec that Mom and I struggled to maintain the life we lived without Dad. Plus, I would still wonder who paid it.

The only other person I knew with that kind of money was Kyle Drekr. But Kyle was the type to *want* me to know that he paid it and that I was not obligated to pay him back - ever. He was always lecturing me about not allowing a man to take advantage. He lived in L.A., so I was sure he'd seen that a lot. It was one of his pinch points over Alec. No matter how loudly I defended him, Kyle believed Alec had taken advantage of a high school senior girl. We'd argued about it repeatedly when Alec first left.

"You don't need him. Let him get his life straightened out first," Kyle had said with a growl.

"We could have stayed friends, even if we waited to date." I'd sniffled out the words.

"He can't be friends with you, Reynolds. Some people can never be *just* friends. I don't think he can control himself around you for very long."

I'd glared at Kyle when he had said that, but secretly I wondered if it were true. I'd fantasized in class that Alec would burst into the room, tell me he loved me, and sweep me up into his arms. Instead, if it hadn't been for extra credit, I would have received a C in English my Freshman year for daydreaming and not participating.

Well, that was over now. Done. Alec had made his choice, and so what if I'd seen him today and already spent too much time dwelling on him? I would move on. My phone rang.

"Molly! You're never going to believe who I saw today."

# CHAPTER TWO

**M**om greeted me at the door of our split-level home wearing a huge smile; her thick blonde hair, cut a bit shorter in layers, framing her beautiful oval face, moved effortlessly around her shoulders. As I wrapped my arms around her and breathed in her peony perfume, I realized just how much I'd missed my mother these last few months. Senior year in college was a time suck.

"Oh, sweetie! You look so good!" Mom wrapped my hair in her hands, pulling my face close to hers to plant a kiss on my forehead. "I'm so happy you're home. Wait until Ben sees you."

"Where is he?" I untangled Mom from my hair and proceeded into the house with my bags.

"Over at Gavin's, but he'll be home in time for dinner. What are you in the mood for? Pizza? Subs? We could go out."

"It doesn't matter. Whatever you want. This last semester required a lot of junk food. I'm actually on a first name basis with the meal delivery guy."

Mom smiled. "Well, tonight, we will celebrate completing your next to the last semester by heading over to Holland's Steakhouse. And tomorrow night, I will cook your favorite - Parmesan Chicken."

"Sounds good," I replied as I made my way down the hall to my room. I noticed the house hadn't changed since I left other than a new tart warmer on the small table at the end of the hall.

"Oh, and before I forget. I'm not going to tell you who, but an old friend is coming to stay for a visit. I told him he could sleep on the sofa bed in the family room downstairs."

"An old friend?" I paused in the doorway to my bedroom. Did she mean Alec? Why would he stay here and not his house? Had he moved away from Locklyn? "Who is it?"

"I'm not going to ruin the surprise. He's already on his way and will probably arrive about the same time as Ben."

"Mom?"

She turned on her heel and waved her hand in the air. "Nope, not telling. Now get ready."

~   ~   ~

Since I wasn't sure who was joining us for dinner, I changed into a black wrap dress and a pair of ankle boots. My common sense told me to wear leggings so I wouldn't freeze, but unfortunately, my flirty sense kicked in and won. Bare legs it was.

When the doorbell rang, I smoothed my dress and calmly announced that I would get it. With my hand on the knob, I took a deep breath. If it was Alec, maybe he thought now was a good time to rekindle what we started four years ago. Perhaps he thought I was finally old enough for him. *Oh, grow up, Girl. You don't need Alec. You are a grown woman.* I opened the door.

"Kyle?"

"Hey, Reynolds! Surprise!" The big man opened the screen door as I stood in utter shock and picked me up into a hug. When I didn't respond, he swung me around like a rag doll until I grabbed his shoulders.

"Kyle, stop! You're going to make me throw up!"

He set me down. "Well, that's better than the look of disgust on your face."

My cheeks heated. "I didn't mean that look for you. I was just shocked to see you at the door."

"Not making it any better. Were you expecting someone else?"

I started to say Alec but bit my tongue. "I didn't know who to expect. What are you doing here? Weren't you in California this morning when I talked to you?"

Kyle climbed the steps to the living room to greet my mom. He dismissed me with a wave when he saw her. "I was already on my way to the airport. Hi, Stella. You're looking as fabulous as always. Stephen's a lucky guy."

Mom gave Kyle a sly smile. "Well, thank you, Kyle. It's nice to hear a compliment from a man who lives in L.A. and sees beautiful women all day long."

"Yeah, well, they're not all actresses." Kyle set his suitcase down in front of the couch as I rolled my eyes. My relationship with Kyle had changed - we were friends now - but he was still infuriatingly Kyle.

"So you came to visit me? What would you have done if I'd decided to surprise you in California?" I asked.

"Let's be honest, Reynolds. You wouldn't have." Kyle turned away from me as the candy dish on the dining room table caught his attention.

Before I could argue with him, the front door opened, and heavy footsteps trudged up the stairs. My teenage brother smiled when he saw me. "Ains! Mom said you would be here." He hugged me, and I was surprised at how much muscle my little thirteen-year-old brother had gained while I was gone. He wore a pair of jeans with an oversized black hoodie with a mop of dark brown curls on his head, a contrast to Mom's and my light blonde hair; undeniable evidence that he was Gerald Reynolds' son.

"Kyle, man!" Ben and Kyle gave each other that manly hug-thing that ended in a fist bump.

"Woah, someone's been hitting the weights." Kyle squeezed Ben's upper arm.

"You can find us at the gym every morning before school," Mom said as she handed Kyle a cold bottle of water.

Kyle's mouth drew into its know-it-all smirk as he playfully shoved Ben's shoulder. "Really? So tell me about the hot girl who works out there every morning."

Ben laughed as he went off to his room to get ready for dinner.

"Hurry up, Ben!" Mom called after him. "Kyle and Ainsley are going to take her car to Holland's, and we're going to follow."

"Oh, okay," I said, clearly uninformed of Mom's plan.

"That way, the two of you can get us a table early," she said. "Is that all right?"

"Of course, Stella," Kyle answered for me as he popped a caramel in his mouth from the candy dish. "I'm starving. Can we leave now, Reynolds?"

~ ~ ~

Holland's Steakhouse was buzzing with sound, people chattering, steak knives and cutlery clanging, and country music blasting a little too loud for a restaurant. I ordered my favorite marinated steak medium rare with a loaded sweet potato and green beans for the obligatory side of healthy.

Mom insisted that she pay for the meal, including Kyle's. Her horror novels had officially hit bestselling status, and she wanted to celebrate her accomplishment as well as me so close to finishing my degree. At first, Kyle argued with her, stating that he wouldn't have ordered such a large steak and appetizers if he'd known she would pay, but as usual, Stella Reynolds won the argument.

As a consolation, Kyle volunteered to buy dessert from the bakery nearby that made the finest and richest cakes in all of Locklyn. No one from the Reynolds family chose to argue with him.

Since I'd agreed to go with Kyle after dinner, I left our table for the restroom while everyone was still enjoying their conversation. After taking care of the basic need to rid my bladder of multiple glasses of iced tea, I reapplied my lip gloss and ran a hand through my thick hair to give it some more volume on top.

As I came out of the restroom, I ran straight into someone, the force knocking me backward and almost into the wall, except that the stranger reached out and caught me before I fell.

"Oh, hello. Are you all right, Miss?"

"Um, yes. I'm sorry. I shouldn't have been in such a hurry." I looked up to see a handsome man with the classic chiseled features of a strong jaw, rugged stubble, and thick dark hair. He was older than me. Probably in his mid to late thirties. It didn't take an expert in men's tailored suits to guess his were expensive.

"No, I apologize. My mind was elsewhere," the man said. I noticed that as he turned his head to allow a young woman to pass us, he subtly took in my outfit from head to toe. "I hope I didn't hurt you."

I smiled up at him. "No. I'm not that fragile."

He surveyed me again, a little less subtle. "I certainly do not think you are fragile. Miss?"

"Reynolds. Ainsley Reynolds."

His eyes suddenly flashed something I couldn't read, and then it was gone. "Miss Reynolds, I will let you go on with your evening." He shifted to the wall so that I could pass. Instead, I thrust my hand out to him. Looking down, he took my hand to shake it.

"You didn't tell me your name." *Please tell me it's Henry Cavill.*

"Ah," he said, withdrawing his wallet and handing me a business card.

I read it out loud. "*The Honorable Rafe Kae.* You're a judge?"

"Yes," he answered, then leaned down near my ear. "I hope that doesn't scare you."

I chuckled. "You would be amazed at what it takes to scare me. I just always pictured judges as old men dressed in black robes."

"I do wear a robe, but I try to leave it at work when I dine out," Rafe smiled down at me. He was about as tall as Kyle, probably six foot three, and from his suit, I would guess at least 240 pounds of muscle.

"Well, I'd better get back to my family. It was nice meeting you, Judge Kae."

The dark-haired man smiled, and I could've sworn his eyes gleamed for a moment, sending a slight shock through me. "Please, it is Rafe. You as well, Miss Reynolds. Perhaps I will see you again."

~ ~ ~

After dinner, Mom and Ben headed home in her car while I drove Kyle down the street to Smith's Cups and Cakes.

"Stephen is coming home this weekend," I said, smiling as we got out of my car in front of the bakery. "Are you planning on sharing the sofa bed with him?"

"Your mom and Stephen don't share the same bed?" Kyle eyeballed me.

"They're Christians, and Stephen is a preacher, so no."

Kyle nudged me with his shoulder once we were on the sidewalk. "Then I guess Stephen better sleep on the left side."

I laughed as I pictured Kyle and Stephen fighting for space on the full-size sofa bed when a shadow emerged from the corner of my eye. I turned and caught a glimpse of a man across the street. He stood rooted to the sidewalk like a marbled statue, watching us. I would have passed on by and shrugged it off as male attention, except there was something odd about him.

It was a bit chilly out this evening, but the man wore no jacket, only khakis, and a tucked-in dress shirt. Was he homeless? It was rare to see homeless in Locklyn as the town prided itself on helping those find shelter and jobs to get back on their feet.

The wind whipped through the street, and the man's brown hair rose with the gusts, yet he still didn't move.

"What's wrong?" Kyle asked when I stopped.

"That man…" I trailed off as the man began crossing the street, heading towards us.

"Do you know him?" Kyle moved in front of me as if to shield me from some blow.

"I don't think so," I whispered. The man came closer, his gaze never leaving mine.

"Ainsley Reynolds," he said in a cracked voice that sounded as if he desperately needed a drink of water. When Kyle put his hand up, the man stopped only two feet away; one foot in the street, one foot on the curb.

"Yes," I answered, peeking over Kyle's giant shoulder.

"I have a message for you. A warning."

"Man, you need to back off," Kyle said, taking a step forward, but something instinctually made me grab his arm to stop him from getting any closer to the man. Something was wrong. Every fiber of my being was on fire, warning me not to take the man lightly. But not to get too close either.

"What is it?"

"You have gotten his attention. He can see you now. He's coming for you – and your family."

Kyle placed his firm hand over my trembling one on his jacket. "Who can see her?"

"Jai-ish."

I shook my head. "Who is Jai-ish?"

"The great general of an army, the one who-" A sound rang out, and the man's head suddenly split into millions of flying chunks, spraying Kyle and me with a mist of blood. I jumped as I realized it had been a gunshot. Kyle pushed me back against the brick wall of the bakery and then shoved me towards the building's front door. Once inside, Kyle began dialing 9-1-1 on his phone and yelling at the people inside the bakery to take cover. I peeked out again through the window, but the street was quiet.

The man's body lay on the street, his arms outstretched to his sides as if nailed to an invisible cross.

# CHAPTER THREE

Alec and I stared at each other until I began to feel a bit uncomfortable. How had we circled back to this? Me standing over a body and Detective Alec Graham investigating the case? Apparently, he'd been off duty when he got the call as he was wearing a pair of jeans and a black leather jacket. His dark green ball cap was pulled down, but I could still make out the focused expression he wore as he observed the crime scene. His eyes scanned my outfit as he crouched near what was left of the man's head, which, thankfully, was covered with several sheets. I tried to ignore the blood soaking through each layer of the fabric. The bakery owner had given Kyle and me wet rags to wash the blood from our faces, but the metallic scent still lingered on our clothes, hair, and heavily in the air.

"I take it you're the one who found the body?"

"No. The man was alive when he approached me, and then someone shot him." I crossed my ankles.

He glanced up at me. "What were you doing here?"

"Buying a cake from the bakery."

"Sounds familiar," he said, referring to the first time I came face-to-face with a demon. His new partner, Detective Anita Wallace, who I'd met briefly a few years ago during the Artist murders, was pushing a gloved hand into the dead man's pockets. Forensics investigators and other officers littered the scene. Alec ordered the bakery cleared since no one inside had seen anything.

When I didn't respond, Alec narrowed his eyes. "Did he say anything to you?"

"Yes." I looked over at his partner and then back to Alec. "But, I'd rather not repeat it right now."

"If I ask you privately, will you tell me?"

"Yes," I answered too quickly and silently chastised my mouth. I bent down near the body, careful not to touch it.

"You may not want to do that."

"In the past four years, I've seen quite a few male bodies," I said quietly. When Alec's eyes flitted over me, I stammered. "Dead bodies. I mean, I've seen quite a few dead bodies. That were male." What was wrong with me? Why was I suddenly bumbling like an idiot?

Alec gave me a half-grin before he went back to studying the body. "Why don't you meet me in the bakery, and we can go over what happened?"

I nodded as I stood. I needed to talk with Kyle and the others. Who was this Jai-ish, and what did he want with my family? A small tremor of fear crept up my spine. Whoever he was, someone was willing to murder a man in the street to keep him from divulging the secret.

~ ~ ~

"Ugh. What's he doing here?" Kyle groaned loudly into my ear as if the detectives standing six feet away at the bakery door couldn't hear him.

I hooked my arm into his, forcing him to lean down to my level. Not that I was short at five-foot-six, but with Kyle, I always felt small.

"Stop it. He's the lead homicide detective in charge of this case. He will kick us out if we don't behave," I whispered.

Kyle ran his other hand through his hair, then frowned. "Well, we need to go home and shower."

I heard someone clear their throat and looked up to see Alec's blank expression meet my quite-startled one.

Kyle nodded his head at Alec. "Detective Graham, it's a pleasure to see you again in this small town. Got your one bullet?"

I cringed at his Barney Fife reference and know-it-all smirk. Except for joking with Ben, it'd been a long time since I'd seen Kyle bust that out.

"Kyle Drekr. What are you doing in Locklyn? Don't you have a T.V. show? Or, did that get canceled?"

I heard Kyle's sharp intake of breath, and I almost laughed. These two still really disliked each other.

"Kyle is staying with me for a few days," I said as I pulled Kyle's arm closer to my body, practically snuggling it. "Plus, we work together on cases like this one."

"Cases like this one? That doesn't bode well." Alec studied us for a moment. "Are you two…together now?"

I opened my mouth but closed it quickly. What could one little white lie do in the scheme of things? I mean, if it made Alec question his decision to leave four years ago…

"How did you guess?" I asked, squeezing Kyle's overly-muscled arm in mine.

Slowly, Kyle turned his unblinking face with its famous fake smile attached to meet my, what I hoped was adoring, gaze. It was much harder than I thought.

*Come on, Kyle, just this once*, I tried to tell him telepathically as I batted my eyelashes up at him.

As if finally receiving my message, Kyle's mouth broke out into a wide grin. I resisted the urge to take a step back. What had I unleashed?

"Yep. It doesn't matter if I'm in L.A. or London. This girl is always calling me back." He squeezed me closer to him. "She started chasing me down last year. She can't get enough of…my charm. You jealous?"

*Good grief.*

Alec raised his eyebrows at us before introducing his new partner and ignoring Kyle's question. The woman seemed in awe of Kyle and his show. Within a few minutes, the conversation had turned from the dead man on the street to the paranormal. She apparently was a raving fan.

"Here, let me give you my card. Just in case," Kyle said to Detective Wallace. "Oh wait," he added, patting his pockets, "it's with my things back at her house."

"Oh, that's okay. Maybe you can just type your number into my phone." The detective handed her phone to Kyle. Alec cleared his throat.

"Here, we can take this outside, Mr. Drekr. Detective Graham would like to question your girlfriend."

Alec nodded toward Kyle. "You could also question *him*." The woman appeared out of sorts, but she mumbled something that sounded like "of course."

Kyle bent down and planted a kiss close to my mouth. "I'll be right back, doll. Don't miss me too hard."

"I'll try not to," I answered, giving him my prettiest smile. Kyle was enjoying this a little too much as he winked at me.

The glass door slammed with a bang after Kyle and Detective Wallace left, and the awkwardness in the empty room became a little too loud. I finally got the courage to look at Alec, who was once again studying me.

"Well, that was painful to watch," Alec remarked.

"What? That Kyle Drekr and I are a couple?"

"That you and Kyle Drekr are *pretending* to be a couple. I'm a detective, Ainsley. And a pretty good one."

"Is that so? Well, Miss Marple, what makes you think we're not a couple?"

Alec took a few steps closer to me, and I could feel all of my frustration with him melting away with the subtle scent of his cologne as he leaned towards my face.

"He didn't kiss you like I would have," he whispered.

My mouth dropped open. "What?"

Alec shrugged as he looked around the deserted bakery again, carefully backing away from me. "It doesn't matter now. Why don't you start from the beginning and tell me what happened tonight?" He scooted a chair out for me at one of the small tables.

I sat down and tried to organize my thoughts while watching him take the chair across from me and pull out his notebook. When his green eyes found mine, I swallowed. This was harder than I thought it would be, sitting this close to him. Now I wished I could have somehow scrubbed the blood off my face without having removed every stitch of makeup.

"We'd gone to dinner at Holland's Steakhouse and then decided to pick up a cake for dessert."

"You and who? Drekr?"

"Yes. Well, Mom and Ben were with us at dinner, but then they drove home."

"So, you and Drekr showed up here, and what happened?"

"We were walking down the sidewalk when I saw the man out of the corner of my eye. He was watching me, so I stopped. That's when he crossed the street."

"Was he carrying anything? Did you feel threatened?"

"He didn't have anything in his hands. I did feel threatened, but not by him."

Alec leaned forward. "What do you mean?"

"I think this falls more in the realm of Seer and Protector than the police, Alec. More of a supernatural problem."

Alec narrowed his eyes. "A dead man is lying in the street. I need to find out who murdered him because a demon certainly didn't shoot him in the head."

I sighed. Alec was right. I wasn't entirely sure this Jai-ish wasn't a human. "Basically, he said I had caught the attention of someone named Jai-ish. He said that my family and I are in danger."

Alec reached across the table and placed his hand over mine. "Ainsley, what do you mean he 'basically' said? I need word-for-word."

"He said, 'You have gotten his attention. He can see you now. He's coming for you - and your family.' When Kyle asked him who, then he answered Jai-ish. But then someone shot him, and we still don't know who this Jai-ish is."

Alec withdrew his hand. "Can Drekr collaborate your story?"

"Of course, but if Kyle thinks this sounds demonic, then he's not going to share details with Detective Wallace."

"I'll pull Drekr aside. Perhaps you shouldn't go anywhere alone until I figure out what we're dealing with."

"I won't be alone. I'm staying at Mom's house for the holidays. Plus, both Kyle and Stephen will be there."

Alec frowned but kept his thoughts to himself. "Try to keep an eye out on Stella and Ben without letting them in on what's happening. I'll call you if I find out anything about this Jai-ish. Is your number the same?"

"I'm surprised you still have it." I stood and started towards the bakery's front door but was stopped short by the tug from Alec's hand on my arm.

"Hey, don't do this." He sounded resigned.

"Don't do what?"

Alec moved around so that he stood in front of me, so close I could smell his familiar cinnamon gum. "Don't shut me out. I'm not your enemy, Ainsley."

"Who are you exactly, Alec? You disappeared from my life, and now, what? You want us to be texting buddies?"

Alec worked his jaw, his eyes appearing darker under the bill of his hat, but I didn't care. I stepped around him. "If you find out anything, you can reach me either on my cell or on Kyle's." I pushed open the door before my courage escaped the confines of my body. Once outside in the cold air, I was thankful that Detective Alec Graham couldn't hear the rapid beating of my heart.

Kyle was still talking to Detective Wallace when I approached, but one look at my face, and I think he knew something had happened inside the bakery. He glanced at someone over my shoulder, and I knew Alec had followed me outside.

Kyle reached his hand out for me, and I took it, allowing him to pull me into his conversation, his arms wrapping around my waist. "Are you all right?" he asked.

"Yes, I'm just ready to go home. Did you call Mom?"

Kyle nodded as he removed his jacket and draped it over my trembling shoulders.

Alec stepped around us. "Drekr, may I speak with you for a minute?"

"Sure," Kyle answered, sounding a bit uneasy.

"I'll be in the car, honey," I said to Kyle, secretly alerting him that I hadn't changed my story about our relationship.

I warmed the car as I waited for Kyle. After a few minutes, he climbed in. "Well, I see he hasn't changed."

"What do you mean?" I asked as I pulled the car into traffic and headed towards home.

"He told me - no, he *ordered* me - to stay with you twenty-four-seven until he figures out who shot our guy."

"Does he know who the man is yet?"

"If he knows, he's not telling us. Why did you tell him we're an item, by the way? Not that it's *not* nice fake-dating you, but it kind of cramps my idea of hitting on Detective Wallace."

"I don't know. It was an impulsive decision. I wanted to rub it in his face that I've moved on. Sorry if you feel used."

"Nah, it doesn't bother me. I'm willing to pretend as long as I can jab Graham. You know I don't like him or the way he was leading you along when you were younger."

I sighed. "He wasn't leading me along. I've told you a million times that Alec wasn't - isn't- like that."

"Agree to disagree. Anyway, it'll be fun making him jealous."

"Let's just keep it reigned in, okay? No on-the-mouth kisses and such."

Kyle grabbed his heart. "You've wounded me. I'll have you know you are the first woman to ever say that to me."

I laughed as I pulled the car into Mom's driveway.

~ ~ ~

My mother accosted us as soon as Kyle and I entered the house, wanting to make sure we were both safe. As soon as he could escape, Kyle took a shower and then went out onto the back deck for "a breath of fresh air" and quietly called Stephen. We needed someone who could check with the organization about any mention of a Jai-ish.

Jai-ish was either a man or a supernatural being. With Alec checking out the human leads and Stephen working on the supernatural side, maybe we would have an answer soon. I'd forgotten to tell Alec that the man had mentioned Jai-ish being the general of an army. Again, it begged the question, what kind of army?

After a long while, I managed to shower and change into flannel pajamas and a heavy cardigan before joining Kyle on the deck. Mom had decided to go to bed, and Ben was in his room. "What did Stephen say?" I asked when Kyle disconnected the call.

"He doesn't recognize the name. He's going to check the archives and maybe talk to Father Mahon about it. He'll call as soon as he has something."

"Is he still coming in this weekend?"

"He didn't say that he's not."

"I forgot to tell Alec that the man said Jai-ish was an army general."

Kyle took a deep breath as he sat down in the Adirondack chair, the cold hardwood creaking under his weight. "Text him."

I blinked. "Did you just tell me to text Detective Graham?"

He rolled his eyes over to me. "You clearly want to, so do it. As your boyfriend, I'll permit it. Just this once."

I stifled a laugh as Ben slid the glass door open. "Did I hear you say you're her boyfriend?" His eyes were wide in shock.

"It's an inside joke," I answered. "Come on. It's freezing out here. Let's go back inside."

"I am," Ben said. "I heard Angel crying to be let in. I didn't know you were even still out here."

"Who's Angel?" Kyle asked as he stood, ready to get inside the cozy house.

"The neighbor's cat. They moved, and I guess, left her behind. I've been bringing her into my room at night. Don't tell Mom. She'd have a fit. She said no more cats."

"Okay, but I didn't see or hear a cat tonight. Are you sure it was her crying?" I asked.

"She just slipped in when I opened the patio door."

I followed Ben to his room to see a very white and very fluffy cat lying on his bed as if she belonged in our house. "She's pretty." I sat down on his bed and petted the long fur. The cat's green eyes sparkled for a moment, and then she leaned back on the bed so I could get her belly.

"She's so cold. She must've been outside all day," I added.

"Yeah, I take her out before Mom sees her in the morning and wait to bring her in at night when Mom goes into her room."

"How old is she?" Kyle asked in a low voice from the doorway.

"I don't know. She seems really old, but when she wants to be held, she scampers around like a kitten." He rubbed between Angel's ears, and she blinked almost lovingly at him.

Kyle stepped into the room and with a quick movement, scooped the cat up into his arms. At first, Angel appeared startled, but after a moment, she began to purr. Kyle took a deep breath and then looked at me.

There was something wrong in his eyes.

After Kyle laid Angel back down on Ben's bed and we said good night to my not-so-little brother, Kyle and I went downstairs to the family room to pull out the sofa.

"What seems odd about that cat?" he asked me as we removed the abundance of overstuffed pillows from this end of the sectional.

"I don't know, what?"

He pulled the frame of the bed out before answering me. "She's dead, Reynolds."

I froze with the set of sheets in my hands. "What? How do you know?"

"I can sense it. Remember Nurse Mattie? It's like that."

He was referring to a ghost at the Ashbury Estate in South Carolina that, thanks to Kyle, I'd come face-to-face with and touched. When Kyle had returned to the renovated Southern mansion one year later, Mattie had moved on. Our assumption was that she had found peace after the missing girls were located within the walls of the Ashbury.

"I mean, the cat was cold, but not dead-flesh cold," I said and shivered. "How is that even possible?"

Kyle shrugged. "I have no idea. I don't see them very often. Maybe a small black dog in an abandoned house. A cat on a windowsill. Eventually, they just disappear into the ether. I don't even know if I would qualify them as ghosts. We can't explain everything, Reynolds. Not until *we* die."

"Wait. If the cat is dead, then how is Ben seeing her?"

Kyle took the sheets from me and raised an eyebrow.

"No," I said, shaking my head. "There is no way Ben's a Seer!" I whispered, afraid Ben might hear me and somehow make the words true.

Kyle calmly began putting the sheets on the mattress. "Why couldn't he be? You are, and so was your dad. It makes sense."

"Maybe you're wrong, Kyle. Maybe Angel isn't dead, just really cold. You're not always right."

Kyle snorted. "Okay. So at some point, without Ben knowing, let the cat out around your mother. If she sees it, then we will know that I was miraculously wrong."

I threw Kyle a dirty look and then left the room as he quietly laughed.

# CHAPTER FOUR

The following day, after I'd showered and dressed, I left my room with the mission of making coffee. It was still early, but Mom and Ben were already up, getting ready to head to the gym.

"You want to join us, Ains?" Ben asked.

"Maybe tomorrow. I've already dressed for the day, and there are some things I need to do. By the way," I lowered my voice, "where is Angel?"

"I put her out on the deck," he whispered back. "She probably took off for the day."

While Ben went back to his room for his phone and earbuds, I meandered over to the patio door and spotted the fluffy tail moving back and forth sporadically on the deck railing. The cat seemed to be watching the birds swoop down in their quest for food. One brave little swallow landed on the bar, not two feet from Angel.

I slid the door open, and the cat turned her head very cautiously in my direction.

"So, you're not coming with us to the gym?" Mom asked as she joined me at the door, her hair pulled up in her famous bun and dressed in a pair of very flattering leggings.

"No, I thought I would work on some stuff for next semester today. Some research for my Capstone project." I focused my eyes on Angel, hoping Mom would look in that direction.

"Okay, well, maybe tomorrow." Finally, she peered out onto the deck. "Well, will you look at that?"

"What is it?" I asked, holding my breath.

"That little bird. What is that? A chickadee or a swallow? I don't know the difference."

"Cat food," I quipped.

Mom patted me on the back. "Oh no, sweetie. There aren't any outdoor cats in the neighborhood. Not since the Robinsons' cat died."

I swallowed. "Did she get hit by a car?"

"No, I think she was just old."

I watched as Angel cleaned her paw with her tongue, took another long look at me, and then resumed her watch on the birds she could no longer catch.

~   ~   ~

I stirred the creamer into my coffee and then took the mug in the living room. I could hear Kyle snoring lightly from downstairs. There was no reason to wake him and confirm he was right about Angel.

And probably right about Ben.

I laid my cell on the end table. Part of me wanted to text Alec and tell him what I'd forgotten. Still, another part of me wanted him to suffer emotionally, which was admittedly an immature part of my psyche.

I picked up my phone. For crying out loud, I would be an elementary school teacher next year. I could handle Detective Graham with the same maturity and responsibility as I did with the students…and the demons. I scrolled to his name. The fact that I still had his number spoke volumes about my willpower.

Me: **I remembered something the man said last night that I forgot to tell you.**

And send.

I set my phone down and waited. There were no dancing bubbles or tiny message that said *read*. I drummed my fingers on the table. It was still early. Maybe he was getting dressed. I didn't even know if he still lived in the same place. What if he was dating someone? Was he married? I hadn't even thought to look for a ring.

Just then, I heard a whistling sound. Or maybe it was more like a hissing. I looked around the living room and dining areas but didn't see anything unusual. The hissing continued.

I followed the sound to the closed door of the main bathroom.

I pushed the door open, then squealed and jumped back. The hose under the toilet had a crack in it, and water was spewing all over the room. I dove in, shielding my face from the water and praying it was clean water and not some sewer water from back up. I needed to get to the valve under the toilet.

My hand found the valve, but no matter how hard I turned - and squealed - I couldn't shut off the water to the toilet.

"What are you doing?" Kyle's voice made me jump. He stood barefoot in the doorway wearing a pair of gray joggers and a matching tee.

"The toilet sprang a leak. I can't get the water off." I grabbed a couple of towels and started mopping up the wet floor.

"I meant the squealing. I could hear you downstairs."

I rolled my eyes as Kyle jumped in front of me and began messing with the valve.

"What is this?! Welded on? Grab me a pair of pliers and a hammer," he barked.

I ran downstairs in my soaked clothes to the storage room and found Dad's toolkit still on the shelf. When I got back to the bathroom, I watched as Kyle, now soaked from his hair to his feet, pulled up the floorboard between the toilet and the bathtub. Lying on his stomach, he reached under the floor, and within a minute, the water finally stopped spewing. I grabbed more towels to soak up the mess.

"I had to turn off the water to the toilet and tub. I don't know what's up with that valve. I can run to Lowe's and see what we need to fix it. I think I may need to replace the whole piece."

I nodded as I pulled at my wet clothes. "I need to change."

"Well, do you think I could use your bathroom then?"

"There's a half-bath downstairs."

"I know, but I need a shower too," he said, taking off his wet tee shirt and holding his arms out to show me his drenched sweats from lying on the floor.

"Oh, okay. Just give me a minute to get dressed. Run those wet towels to the washer and toss them in."

Twenty minutes later, while ignoring Kyle's dry clothes that he must have laid on my bed while I was in the bathroom, I emerged, dressed in a pair of dark jeans, a tight vintage tee, and my favorite thick cardigan. I pulled my still damp hair up into a bun.

"Kyle, thank you for that! Maybe getting it turned on will be-" I was just slipping my ballet flats on as I came through the hall when I spotted Kyle leaning his shoulder against the living room wall, giving me a weird look that made me stop talking.

"What is it?"

Kyle jerked his head to the right, and a figure moved away from the picture window. A man dressed in gray pants and suit jacket turned to look at me with an expressionless stare.

"Alec, what are you doing here?"

Alec's eyes flitted from me to the half-naked and still wearing wet sweatpants Kyle. Kyle puffed his chest out. "If you've got this, doll, then I'm heading to the shower." He moved down the hall to my room. "Oh, and you're more than welcome. Anytime."

I bit my lower lip as I looked back at Alec. He was watching Kyle's back as it disappeared into my bedroom.

"Did you find something out?" I asked since Alec still hadn't answered me. I walked past him to the end table to retrieve my cup of now cold coffee. I took a sip and made a face.

"I got your message this morning, but when you didn't answer my text, I decided to drop by." His voice sounded gravely, and I turned to face him. He looked a bit lost, like he wanted to say more but didn't have the words.

I swallowed. Was I making him miserable? I mean, that had been my intention, but deep down, it really wasn't. I picked up my phone and read his message back to me.

Alec: **What did you forget to tell me?** Then two minutes later: **Are you there? Are you all right?** Then another two minutes later: **I'm on my way to your house.**

I set my phone back down on the table.

"I didn't see your messages. Something happened in the bathroom, and I needed to change clothes. Can I make you some coffee? I could use another cup."

Alec nodded as he followed me into the kitchen. "So, that's why Drekr answered the door wet? He said you were still in the bathroom getting dressed."

I winced. It sounded like Kyle had worded it to make Alec jealous, as was our plan, and now, of course, a very shirtless, very wet Kyle had gone into my room to take a shower.

I made Alec's coffee using a dark roast coffee pod and served it to him plain the way I remembered. He took the mug from my hand, and for a moment, our fingers brushed. Instead of letting go of the cup, however, I looked into his green eyes.

"The main bathroom toilet sprung a leak, and I got drenched. I changed clothes, and Kyle asked if he could use my bathroom to shower before he got dressed because he turned off the water to the main bathroom. That's all there is."

His eyes searched mine. "You don't have to explain."

I let go of his mug and turned to make my own much-needed cup. "I know. It's just that I do feel the need to explain to you why Kyle was half-dressed when you arrived."

"You didn't know I was coming over," he said as he lowered his voice. "Plus, I remember spending a few minutes with you once in the hallway in front of your room. If that's what you and Drekr have, then who am I to judge?"

I snuck a peek at him out of the corner of my eye.

Of course, I remembered that one time he'd kissed me in the hallway right before my mother had come home and almost busted us. I thought about it often because, frankly, no one had satisfied me with a kiss like that since. I took a deep breath.

He took a sip of his coffee. Watching me, he asked, "So, what is it you forgot to tell me last night?"

I stirred my creamer into my mug and then motioned for Alec to join me at the table.

"The man mentioned that Jai-ish was the general of an army. Actually, he said that he was a great general. Now I don't know if he meant an army unit as we know it or something supernatural. Stephen doesn't recognize the name, but he's going to check the archives."

Alec took another sip of his coffee as he listened.

"I thought maybe that might help you narrow down who this Jai-ish might be. Maybe check military records?"

He set his cup down on the table. "The man shot was Mark Tahl, a Religious Studies Professor at the University of North Carolina at Chapel Hill. No military record, no criminal record; not even a speeding ticket."

"He was never in trouble, and yet someone wanted him dead?"

"Looks that way."

"Don't mind me," Kyle's voice rang through the house. I could hear him descending the stairs to the family room. "I'm just getting my shoes."

I pressed my lips together. "Kyle is staying in the family room. Stephen usually sleeps there, but I think he is going to take the living room couch this week."

"Oh," Alec said. He seemed to take his time digesting this new piece of information. Finally, he took another drink of his coffee and then stood. "I should be going. I need to meet up with Detective Wallace and check out your lead on this Jai-ish."

"Okay." I followed Alec to the front door. I wanted to say something else, but I didn't know what to say. The only words in my head were *desperate much, Ainsley?*

I stepped out onto the concrete porch with him. "So, you'll let me know if you find out anything?"

He stopped at the bottom of the steps and looked back up at me. "Yes. Make sure you contact me about anything Stephen learns."

He started to turn away until my mouth overrode my brain, and the words tumbled out. "I'm glad it's you."

He looked back at me questioningly.

"I mean, I'm glad it's you investigating this case." I sat down on the top stair, the cold concrete sending chills through me. I lowered my eyes before I lost my nerve. "I was hoping I'd see you again. I was angry and hurt, but…I did miss you."

Alec's shoes moved closer to the steps, so I raised my eyes to see him leaning down to my eye level. "I missed you too," he said, his voice gravely again. Then he straightened. "You should go back inside before you catch cold. I'm sure Drekr is looking for you."

"We're not together," I said, much too quickly, the words tumbling out faster and faster. I stood and quickly darted down the steps to stand in front of Alec. He took a step backward. "Kyle is my friend. I wanted you to think I'd moved on. I haven't had the time or the inclination to date around. I made Kyle agree to be my fake boyfriend, so maybe you would think I didn't need you. It was wrong, I know, I just-"

"Ainsley. Ainsley, stop," Alec interrupted me. His eyes were wide. I'd shocked him with my immature confession. He probably thought I was a certifiable nutcase now. I'd gone from calm and collected and grown up to a rambling idiot.

He sighed. "Ainsley, I never thought you and Kyle Drekr were a couple. I told you that. Face it, that's just insane." He half-smiled, and my heart melted. "But I really do need to get to work, so I can find out who wanted Mark Tahl dead and why he would risk his life to get a message to you."

He glanced behind me at the front door before meeting my gaze again. "Please keep Drekr with you at all times until we learn something. By the way, where are your mother and Ben?"

"At the gym."

"I'll call Henry and make sure everything is fine there. But try to keep a closer eye on them until I can ascertain if this is a legitimate threat to your family." He started to reach up and touch a tendril of my hair that had worked loose, but instead, he pulled back. "I have to go."

I stood on the driveway with the crisp breeze whipping my legs through the thin denim material as I watched Alec climb into an unmarked black SUV and drive away. But before turning around to join Kyle in the house, something white caught my eye. It was over the small hill from our home towards the main road. I watched as the white thing bobbed up and down. It was at least ten seconds before I realized the white something was a pom-pom decorating the top of a white toboggan pulled down over the black hair of a waif of a girl as she walked quickly down the street towards the heart of town. There was something about her, wrapped in her too-big white puffy jacket with her long hair hanging down the front. She moved quickly as if on a mission, a full backpack strapped to her. Perhaps because I'd never seen her before, she held my attention a little too long until she walked out of my field of vision. I frowned.

There was something troubling about her, but I couldn't put my finger on it.

"Honey, your coffee is getting cold," Kyle's voice carried from the front door to the spot where I stood at the end of my driveway.

I rolled my eyes.

# CHAPTER FIVE

Stephen leaned back on the couch in the living room as my mother scooted in next to him. She reminded me of a little bird nestled into the wings of its parent. Stephen made her feel safe, and I knew without a doubt that the man would give up his life to keep her that way. He'd made the trip to North Carolina from West Virginia a few days early after I'd called him about someone needing to watch over Mom and Ben. The truth was, without locking down the house, there was no way I could keep tabs on both of them at all times *and* stay under Kyle's watchful eye too.

I did feel better now that Alec and I weren't playing some game I'd made up in my head. Kyle was thrilled that he didn't have to pretend to be my loving boyfriend, and he was free to pursue Detective Wallace. As soon as I'd told him the gig was up, he'd been on the phone texting the female detective about a possible dinner out one night this week.

I pulled my legs up into the recliner and scrolled through my social media, although I didn't see any of the updates. Stephen had found something in the archives and wanted to share it with us. Ben was staying over at Gavin's. As soon as Mom went to sleep, Stephen, Kyle, and I would meet in the family room. He said the news was so critical that he'd called Alec.

"Ainsley, are you sure you feel comfortable with Alec coming to join us for a movie? It was Stephen's idea." Mom placed a hand on Stephen's knee.

"Yeah, Mom, it's fine. He's the detective who is investigating the case involving the man Kyle and I saw shot. We've talked, and we're…better now."

Stephen and I exchanged glances. Kyle had filled him in on my original plan to make Alec jealous, which warranted a Stephen-frown, and I had to confess that I'd told Alec the truth. Stephen had been quiet, but I felt that he would give me his opinion at some point. Stephen always liked Alec; he'd just thought the timing was poor when Alec and I tried to grow closer four years ago.

"Plus, I think he's bringing the pizza," Kyle said as he came into the living room with a couple of bottles of water. He dropped one into my lap before crossing the room again and stretching out onto the loveseat. "If you ever get tired of Stephen, maybe dating Graham wouldn't be a bad idea, Stella. I mean, free pizza." He winked at her.

"Kyle," Mom rolled her eyes as she laughed.

Stephen shook his head. "I don't think Stella is the right Reynolds woman for him," he said, looking at me. I shifted in my chair. Thankfully, the doorbell rang.

"Sounds like the pizza is here," Kyle said, rolling his head in my direction. "Do you want me to get it?"

I was already up and crossing the room. I shoved his blond head away from me as I passed the loveseat. "No, but maybe he brought Detective Wallace."

Kyle playfully growled. "Oh, Anita, my love!"

As I descended the stairs to the front door, I heard Mom asking questions about Anita Wallace. I opened the door to see Alec holding two large pizzas.

"Well, I would say it's terrific to see you, but you might think I was referring to the pizzas," I said as I took the oversized boxes from him.

Alec's eyes flitted quickly over my outfit before he answered. I'd spent extra time choosing something that would look casual but catch his eye at the same time. I decided on sapphire blue yoga pants with a matching fitted tee shirt and a long, open, lightweight sweater. "Are you sure you want me here?" he asked in a low voice.

I stopped with one foot on the stair. Stephen and Mom were sitting on the couch against the railing right above us. Granted, the television was on, but neither were hard of hearing. "Yes, of course. It's important," I answered in a whisper.

Alec nodded and followed me up. As I set the pizzas on the table, I heard Mom's voice. "Alec Graham! I must say I'm surprised to see you here, but you look great." I turned to see my mother give Alec a quick hug, and then she introduced him to Stephen. Mom still had no idea that Stephen, Kyle, and I belonged to an organization that searched for and expelled demons. She didn't know about all of us, including Alec, taking the trip to South Carolina four years ago to defeat a demon cluster. As far as she was concerned, this was the first time Alec had met Stephen and that he'd only just met Kyle yesterday in front of the bakery.

"Nice to see you again, Detective Graham," Kyle smiled as he stood to shake Alec's hand.

"You can call me Alec," Alec answered as the two men shook hands. At any moment, I expected a bell to ring and the fight to begin. It wouldn't be the first time the two had had a physical altercation.

"Alec, do you want to help me get the plates?" I asked.

"Sure." After he shed his black jacket and hung it on the back of one of the dining room chairs, he followed me into the kitchen. Thankfully, we kept the plates in the far corner cabinet away from the two doorways to the kitchen. "This is awkward."

I handed him a stack of plates. "I know, but Stephen said what he learned is critical, and we can't talk about anything until Mom goes to bed. Thanks for coming."

With my back to the corner of the counter, the only thing separating me from Alec was the stack of plates he held between us. He wore dark jeans and a fitted gray tee shirt that somehow made him look more rugged. He *had* been working out. He was almost as big as Kyle. I took a deep breath.

He studied my face before he spoke. "This is harder than I thought it would be, Ainsley."

"What do you mean?"

"Seeing you again. Being this close to you again." He took a step away from me, a pained expression crossing his face. "You've grown into a gorgeous woman."

"Oh. Well, thank you. Do you want to do this another night? Would that be easier? I could call you with Stephen's findings."

He shook his head. "No, Stephen said on the phone that it was a matter of life and death."

"What? He didn't tell me that."

Alec shrugged as he took the plates out to the table. *Why hadn't Stephen told me it was life and death?*

~ ~ ~

It was four hours and two movies later before Mom announced that she really must go to bed. She got up way too early to stay up so late. We said good night to her, and Stephen walked her to her bedroom as Alec, Kyle, and I went downstairs to the family room. The sofa bed was closed into its sectional position, making it easier for us to sit spaced apart.

It *had* been awkward, as Alec had said in the kitchen. Before the movies started, Kyle had moved into the recliner so that Alec and I could sit on the loveseat. Still, Alec stayed so close to his end that if he'd actually laughed during the movie, he might have fallen over the armrest and onto the floor.

Now he sat on the very end of the sectional facing the door, perhaps planning his escape. Did it bother him so much having me in the same room? What was worse was that I was acutely aware that Kyle and Stephen had noticed. They'd both seen us four years ago when we had, sort of, a relationship. Now Alec acted like if we got too close, we might burst into flames. Yet, why had he made those flirty comments the other night? Maybe it was because he thought I'd been in a relationship with Kyle.

I sat down in the middle of the sectional, and Kyle, being Kyle, plopped down next to me, swung his legs onto the sectional, and threw his head onto my lap. I pushed him off, which only made him laugh.

Alec's face remained blank.

It was at least ten minutes before Stephen joined us in the family room.

"Dude," Kyle started, but after a glare from Stephen, Kyle shut his mouth.

The preacher stood in front of the television as if addressing his congregation. "I called Maren today on my drive here and filled her in. She would have come this evening, but that would've caused your mother to ask too many questions." He looked at me. "We need to discuss bringing Stella into this."

"I don't want Mom and Ben to know anything about this. If Dad had wanted that, then he would've told them."

Kyle reached over and touched the back of my hand. "Gerald was wrong. He knew you were the Seer, and he should've told you. Stephen is marrying your mother. We can't keep all of this from her with everyone practically living here."

Stephen cleared his throat. "Kyle is right, Ainsley. *I* don't want to keep this from her."

I exhaled. "I understand. Spouses shouldn't keep secrets from each other."

"So, it's agreed. You and I will sit down with Stella tomorrow."

"Tomorrow?"

Stephen went to the recliner near Alec and sat. "The sooner, the better. There is something I found in the archives that changes everything."

"You said it was a matter of life and death," Alec said.

Stephen took a deep breath and let it out slowly. "Jai-ish was the general of an army of fallen angels. He is what Kyle would call a 'next level' demon. He is more powerful than your common Muladach or demon cluster."

"Has he ever been expelled back to Hell before?" Kyle asked.

Stephen leaned forward and glanced at Alec. Alec's jaw clenched, and I wondered if Stephen had told Alec more on the phone than he let on. Finally, Stephen looked at Kyle and me.

"Every time a Seer has come up against Jai-ish, they've died."

The silence in the room was palpable. After a few moments, Kyle spoke softly, "How did they die?"

"Their hearts stopped. They dropped dead on site."

I swallowed. "Do we have records of the expulsions? Maybe we can study those and come up with a new plan. Something the other Seers didn't know."

Stephen gave me a small smile. "That's not a risk we're willing to take."

"Who's we?" Kyle asked, frowning. "Because I didn't know about any of this."

"The organization, Malus Navis. Ainsley, you are the best Seer the organization has ever had. You are more powerful than even Gerald, which I didn't think was possible. The organization won't risk you confronting Jai-ish." He narrowed his eyes at me. "And as your future stepfather, I won't risk losing you."

Alec cleared his throat, his jaw still tightly clenched. "Mark Tahl told Ainsley and Kyle that Jai-ish had seen her. He's coming after her and her family. What if he confronts her?"

"Father Mahon and a few of the other leaders believe that there is a blessed object that might 'hide' Ainsley from Jai-ish. Eventually, the demon might move on when he can no longer see her."

"There are no such things as blessed objects," Kyle said, standing and pushing his hands through his hair. "Only people who have the power already." He crossed his arms over his chest and turned his back to us as he stood under the television mounted on the wall.

"You and I disagree about this all the time, Kyle," Stephen said with a sigh.

"But believing in the object is better than going in unprepared, right?" Alec asked, directing his question to Kyle's back.

"But that's just it," I answered. "I wouldn't be going in at all. I'd be hiding for the rest of my life, afraid to tackle even one demon in case Jai-ish saw my power blinking like a searchlight. I would rather place my faith in God, and in the power He's given me than in some material object."

Stephen brought his steepled hands together to his mouth, nodding his head and seriously contemplating what Kyle and I were saying. I looked at Alec, who was staring through me, his eyes glazed over in deep thought.

"Ainsley, at the risk of riling you up," Alec said slowly. "You're young, just twenty-two. I don't think you realize that you will die if you try to expel this demon."

My first instinct was to get angry, but I pushed that emotion down. Instead, I scooted over to him on the couch and pulled his hand into mine. He inhaled sharply.

"Alec, when you joined the Marines and deployed the first time, did you know you might die if you faced the enemy?"

"Yes, but only intellectually. I didn't have the realization of my finiteness until men around me started dying. Friends. Even now," Alec said as he squeezed my hand, "I know I could die doing my job any day."

"But you still do it to protect people you don't know. This is for Mom and Ben, Alec. If I were to give up my life for anyone, it would be my friends and family." I searched his eyes. I wanted to add, "I'd do it for you," but that sentence seemed too intimate to share in front of Kyle and Stephen.

Kyle turned around, and I could read the fury in his eyes, but he kept his voice low and restrained. "Stephen, get us the records of the past attempts. Let us go over them. All of us need to pray for protection and invisibility over Ainsley in the meantime."

I nodded. "And protection and invisibility over Mom and Ben, too. We will tell Mom everything tomorrow."

Alec, who still held my hand, squeezed it again. "Are you sure? Are you sure you can do this?"

I managed to turn my lips up into a smile as I nodded. Was I sure? No, not totally. Was I scared? Terrified. Did I have faith in God? Absolutely. Did I have faith in myself?

That's what worried me.

# CHAPTER SIX

The four of us prayed, and I felt an incredible breeze rush into the family room, pushing around and through me. I knew it was the Holy Spirit, and by the time I walked Alec outside to his truck, I knew I had God's protection covering me.

Alec stopped when he reached the truck, turning slowly to face me. The streetlight was on, and I could see the worry etched across his face. "Do you want me here tomorrow when you tell your mother?"

"No, that's okay. She's probably going to be angry that so many people are involved in something that she didn't know anything about. I just hope that she still wants to marry Stephen."

"I didn't think about that. You Reynolds women do hold onto anger," he said as he grinned at me.

"Haha. Speaking of holding onto things," I said as I lightly shoved his shoulder. "Why did you act like I was a leper tonight during the movies?"

He looked down at the concrete driveway for a second before meeting my stare. "I don't know how to handle this. When I'm around you, I remember how it felt to be caught up with you; the way you would look at me like I could do anything, how your hair felt in my hands, the awkward way you reveal things, the sound of your laugh. When I realized that we couldn't be anything, it broke my heart. It was easier to stay away from you the last few years than to try to be your friend."

"And you don't want to feel that heartache again."

His jaw clenched. "No, I don't."

"Well, I don't either. It's a painful and yet, empty and numb feeling. I mean, how is that even possible? To feel nothing and everything at the same time?"

Alec slowly took my hand. "I don't know."

I smiled up at him as I took a step closer. Maybe it was all the talk of me possibly dying for the people I loved, but my courage grew. "But you know what? I would rather risk feeling like that again than never having loved you. You wanted me to have a life, to have fun, to date other guys. Instead, I compared every man I met to you. After tonight, no matter what happens, I want you to know that what I felt for you wasn't a schoolgirl crush. It wasn't because we were in a series of dangerous and extraordinary events. It was real. You're right - you and I can never be just friends. But it's always been you. When I close my eyes, you are the only one I see. We can never joke around the way Kyle and I do because although I admittedly love Kyle, I've never been *in love* with him-"

Alec's mouth suddenly crashed over mine, and for a moment, that familiar sensation of the world slipping away threatened to swallow me whole. Alec's hand moved up to the back of my neck as he pulled me closer to him. Breathing him in, I was vaguely aware of the cold air - after all, it was almost 4am on a December morning. I guess sensing the cold, Alec turned me closer to the SUV, shielding me from the wind as he wrapped his arms around me.

After a few minutes, he rested his lips on my forehead. "I should go before your neighbors wake up and see us. Call me after you tell Stella about everything."

Alec started to turn away, but I pulled him back and kissed him one more time. I leaned back to see his surprised but pleased expression. "I'm tired of wanting to kiss you and not being able to."

"Me too," he whispered as he tugged lightly on my high ponytail, which led to another kiss. Then another. And another.

~   ~   ~

I slept very little in the early morning hours, my mind bouncing between finally kissing Alec again to telling Mom about the organization and Dad's secret and to what might happen if I come up against Jai-ish. Finally, with a great deal of effort, I dragged myself from my warm comforter to the shower, allowing the hot water to ease some of the tension and force my shoulders away from my ears.

I took my time getting dressed and even blew my hair dry before braiding it to one side in a "fishtail" braid. I'd chosen a pair of black skinny jeans and a rose gold V-neck sweater. As per my custom in recent years, I tossed on a pair of funny-looking socks – a black pair with images of tiny bananas.

By the time I left my bedroom, Mom, Stephen, and Kyle were at the dining table with coffee and donuts.

"Where did those come from?"

"I brought them." Alec's voice carried from the kitchen, and I turned to see him with a coffee mug in one hand and a saucer in the other.

"What time is it?" I asked, perplexed. It had been after 4am before Alec left this morning, and I had slept fitfully.

"Ten," Kyle answered, running his hand through his highlighted blond hair, clearly still tired. "Some of us don't sleep all day."

Mom pushed the box of donuts towards me. "Well, you look beautiful, sleepyhead."

I thanked Mom and ignored the box of wonderfully tempting treats. My guess was the men had decided this morning was the best time to drop the bombshell on Stella Reynolds.

Alec watched me make my coffee at the Keurig and retrieve a bottle of sugar-free Sweet Cream creamer from the refrigerator in the kitchen. "If I'd known when you were gonna get up, I would'a made you a cup." I could hear the undercurrent of his Southern accent. It stayed hidden most of the time, but every once in a while, it slipped out in the most delightful sound, making his voice sound rugged and country.

"If I'd known the three of you were going to ambush my mother with donuts, I would have gotten up earlier," I whispered. Apparently, Alec and Stephen texted regularly now. I scolded myself. That was unfair. Stephen had kept up with Alec throughout the years, especially when Alec became a new Christian and needed encouragement and advice.

"Stephen wanted to get it over with," Alec whispered back.

"Hmm," was all I could say as I moved into the dining area. Mom smiled up at me as I slid into the chair closest to her. *Oh God, please. She is so happy with Stephen. Please don't let this news upset her so severely that she breaks the engagement. We need Stephen in our lives.*

"Ainsley, are you all right? Your eyes look glazed over." Mom patted my arm.

"I'm fine. Just a little tired." I snuck a peek at Stephen, who was frowning into his mug.

"So, do you two have plans today?" Mom asked me.

"What?"

"I assumed since Alec was here that you two had made plans. I'm not blind, Ainsley."

My eyes darted to Stephen again, and I shook my head. Maybe now wasn't the best time to confess everything to her. Stephen only frowned a little deeper.

Stephen cleared his throat and reached for Mom's hand – the hand that wore the beautiful diamond engagement ring. "Stella, I love you. I love you so much. But there is something I have to tell you."

Mom's eyes grew wide. Waves of fear radiated off her and onto me. She and I were closer than I knew.

"Is it Ben? Has something happened to Ben?" Mom's voice cracked.

This time I placed my hand on her denim-clad thigh. "No, Mom. Ben is fine. This is about Dad. And me." I took a deep breath. "And Stephen."

"What? I don't understand." Mom's neat brows furrowed, and I wanted to hug her. I wanted to tell her this was just a big joke. Alec sat down in the chair at the end of the table. Kyle remained quiet across from Mom.

"Do you remember when Gerald used to go on the occasional business trip out of town?" Stephen asked.

Mom turned her head from me to him. "Yes," she answered slowly.

"Those weren't business trips with the plant. The trips were sanctioned through an organization called Malus Navis. I'm a member, and so is Kyle."

Mom looked from Stephen to Kyle and back again. "Is this a club? Like the Moose?"

Stephen smiled. "No, not really. It's an organization that seeks out demonic activity and expels the demons back to Hell."

Mom laughed. "Oh my gosh, Stephen! You had me going for a second. Maybe *you* should write horror novels."

"Mom?" I moved my hand from her leg to her upper arm to get her attention. She turned to look at me, her blonde spiral curls tumbling around her shoulders. "Stephen isn't joking. He and Dad worked together on certain demonic cases. That's how they met Kyle."

By her raised eyebrow, Mom was still skeptical.

"Stella?" Alec leaned forward in his chair slightly. "Remember four years ago when I was investigating the case with the serial killer known as The Artist?"

"Of course," Mom's tone of voice sounded sober now.

"Ainsley came to me because she'd seen a demon whispering to the woman she later found dead. She was seeing the demons influencing the man killing those people. I didn't believe it either at first, but then I saw something on a video that changed my mind. Then I met Stephen and some others from Malus Navis. It's the truth, Stella."

Mom searched Alec's face, probably looking for the lie. She turned to Stephen and withdrew her hand from his.

"Gerald would have told me if he belonged to something like that."

Stephen swallowed. "He didn't tell you. He felt it was in your best interest if he kept it to himself. Gerald suspected Ainsley of having the gift to discern spirits, but he didn't get the chance to share it with her before he passed away. I know because he and I talked about it."

Mom let out an exasperated sigh. "So, you all belong to this club or organization or whatever it is? You've been doing this *thing* for *years* and have just now decided to tell me?"

I bit my tongue from explaining to the three men that this was the famous Reynolds temper that they'd only seen glimpses of in me. Stella was a whole lotta wrath.

"To protect you," Stephen said, reaching for Mom's hand, but she withdrew it out of his reach and placed it on her lap.

"Stella, truth is, you weren't in a position to understand a few years ago," Kyle said, his upbeat attitude gone. "You didn't believe in much when I met you. Not until you called Stephen about going to church."

"I only called Stephen because I dreamt…" her voice trailed off as her gaze landed on the portrait on the living room wall of our family before Dad died. We all knew the rest of that sentence. Mom had dreamt of Dad telling her to call Stephen about a church. She'd called Stephen, who had made a trip to North Carolina and promptly fell in love with her. Probably part of Dad's plan.

"It wasn't a dream, Mom. It was a visitation. He visited me in my dream the same night while I was in South Carolina."

Her eyes widened.

"Mom, it's more than that. There is a new threat to us right now. A threat greater than a normal demon."

"A greater threat than a demon?" Mom sounded incredulous.

Kyle cleared his throat. "Stella, there is a demon higher up on the hierarchy who has taken notice of

Ainsley. See, your daughter can not only sense the demons; she has the power to expel them. She can see trapped spirits and free them. She can travel between this realm and the next. She's what we call a Seer. That's what Gerald was. This demon is targeting her."

"Stella," Alec said. "The man that was shot the other night was a professor of Religious Studies. He was trying to warn Ainsley that she, and you and Ben, are in danger."

"Gerald was a Seer," Mom stated to no one in particular.

"Yes."

"And you're a Seer?" she asked me.

"Yes."

"And you?" she asked Kyle.

"I'm what they call a Protector. I can see and hear demons and trapped spirits. When I'm in the presence of a Seer, I can move between the realms and help amplify the Seer's powers to protect them from an attack. I worked with Gerald when I was a teenager. I was his Protector. Now I'm Ainsley's."

"And you?" Mom whispered to Stephen, her eyes blinking.

"I assist with the investigations. Over the past four years, I've worked specifically with Ainsley and Kyle. The demons usually influence a human to do things. I help to find out who the person is so we can stop him or her."

"I guess you do something with them too?" Mom asked Alec, and I could see the tears building in her eyes.

Alec shook his head. "Not like that. I'm only involved because there was a murder in Locklyn, and I'm the lead homicide detective."

Mom nodded her head. "Well, that explains why you were so headstrong about talking to Alec four years ago. You couldn't tell anyone what you saw, could you?"

"No," I answered. "I didn't know about Dad. Maren Bell told me."

"Maren Bell?"

"The Psychology teacher at the high school, remember her?"

"Of course, she grew up with Stephen." Mom looked back at him. "Is she one too?"

Stephen frowned. "Maren isn't a Seer or a Protector. She only works with us to ensure that the person suspected of being influenced by demons doesn't have a mental disorder instead."

"I see." Mom rose from her chair. "I'm going to go lie down for a while. I need to think about this."

"Stella," Stephen said as he started to stand.

She whirled on him. "No, I want to be alone right now. I need to think about why you are really here. I thought it was because of me, but maybe it's because you need to keep a close eye on Ainsley and Kyle. Maybe that's the *only* reason."

"That's not the only reason." Stephen followed her down the hall, Mom's footsteps turning into stomps. "Come on, Stella, Ainsley hasn't even been here when I've visited you. She's been at college."

The bedroom door slammed.

"Stella, I'm here because I love you. I gave you that ring because I love you. This thing that we do is to help people. There are only so many Seers and Protectors in the world. Gerald knew that, and that's why he only took on the most difficult cases."

The house grew quiet. Alec, Kyle, and I exchanged glances as I took a drink of my coffee. It was heartbreaking.

"Stella, please open the door. Talk to me." Stephen's voice cracked.

"Maybe the three of us should drive over to my place to talk and give them some time alone," Alec suggested.

"Yeah, sounds good." Kyle popped the last bite of donut into his mouth as he stood.

As we passed through the living room, I peered down the hall. Stephen had his back against Mom's bedroom door, sitting on the floor with his knees pulled up and head down. I motioned for Alec and Kyle to go on to the truck. I went to Stephen and knelt in front of him, my hand on his knee.

"It'll be okay," I whispered to him. "Mom's hurt, but she loves you, and she knows that Ben and I love you." When he raised his head, tears were streaming down his face. I hugged him before leaving with Alec and Kyle.

~ ~ ~

"Do you think Maren can get us the archives about Jai-ish?" Kyle asked after we were in Alec's SUV.

"Maybe, if they are digital now. Will you call her?" I buckled my seatbelt in the front seat.

Alec started the engine. "How did Stephen look?"

"Upset, heartbroken, miserable. All the things. I think Mom just needs to sort out her feelings. This was a lot to throw at her all at once. She just learned that Dad, her first love, kept a huge secret from her. Then to make it worse, *we* kept the same secret from her."

"Do you think she will give Stephen another chance?"

I took a deep breath and let it out, thinking about Mom's options and knowing her. "Yes, I do. If she weren't planning on it, she would have asked him to leave. She would've probably asked both of you to leave too."

"Why me?" Kyle asked, shocked that Stella might have considered tossing him out.

"Just because you are part of this. I'm afraid of what she will say to Maren if she sees her again." Maren had helped me the first time I'd seen demons in Locklyn, which led her to lie to my mother, pretending to give me counseling sessions to be able to talk freely with me about the Muladach.

Alec turned the truck onto his street. "Maren is also the one who risked her life in Charlotte so you could find me and stop the Artist. That will mean something to Stella once she knows the truth. Once she allows Stephen to tell her everything."

He parked the SUV in front of his small brick house, and we got out and headed for the front porch.

"You still live here. I wondered if you had moved. I could never bring myself to drive down Lanier Lane and check."

Alec didn't answer as he opened the glass door and inserted his house key into the lock.

"Frankly, I thought it would be bigger. I heard about the size of your grandfather's place," Kyle remarked, looking down at the chairs on the porch.

"Like your place?" Alec asked him as he swung the door open.

Kyle laughed and walked inside to the living room. "My place is in L.A. Of course, it's big with lots of steel and glass. This is…homey."

"Well, I've always loved it. It's cozy," I said as I reached up and turned Alec's face towards me and gave him a quick kiss on the cheek. He smiled.

"It's paid for," he said. "Can I get you something to drink?"

"Bottled water, if you have it," Kyle said, sitting down on the leather couch. "I'm going to try to call Maren again."

Alec tossed a bottle of water to Kyle, and we waited while he tried to call Maren. Alec and I moved into the kitchen in the back of the house when she finally answered the phone.

"Everything still looks the same," I said as I leaned against the kitchen counter, remembering the morning that Alec made us eggs and bacon at the stove.

A look came into Alec's eyes as he moved in front of me, leaving little space between us. He leaned down, encircling my waist in his hands. "I know. It desperately needs a woman's touch," he growled into my ear before brushing his lips over mine.

"You know," Kyle said, stepping down into the kitchen and interrupting us. "This place may be on the smaller side from the outside, but the rooms are rather large on the interior. The builders made the most use of the space." He glanced around the kitchen. "If you took out this counter in the middle of the room and moved it to along this wall, it would open up this whole room."

Alec half-smiled as he moved away from me. "I'll think about it. What did Maren say?"

"She said she can download the digital archives and send them to me today. She also said, 'Oh Crap!' in her West Virginia accent when I told her Stephen told Stella everything."

"Well, not everything," I remarked. "Alec, can I make coffee?"

"Sure, and there's pizza in the fridge."

Kyle made a beeline for the refrigerator while I started making a pot of coffee.

Alec sat down in one of the kitchen chairs across the room. "There's also coffee creamer in there too."

"I thought you liked your coffee black and strong enough to grow hair," I teased.

"I do. I picked it up for you," he said with a smile.

"For me?!" Kyle asked with mock surprise in a falsetto voice, backing out of the refrigerator with a slice of pizza and a bottle of sugar-free chocolate caramel creamer.

I shoved him away as I took the bottle. "I do not talk like that!"

Kyle continued in the high-pitched voice. "Oh, Alec! Thank you!"

Alec only shook his head as he perched his legs up on one of the other chairs. In the past, Kyle had had a lot of anger issues and combined with Alec's jealous nature, they'd come to blows once. It was good to see them getting along. I guessed all three of us had changed over the years.

As I waited for the pot of coffee to brew, Kyle's phone dinged. "Looks like Maren is getting the job done," he said, glancing down at his phone as it continued to beep. He looked up at me from the table. "I'll download them as they come in, but it seems there are a lot of entries for this Jai-ish."

"Well, maybe that will give us an advantage," I said, turning away to face the coffee pot. My voice sounded strong. I sounded courageous, but my insides were full of uncontrollable tremors.

I set three mugs down on the kitchen table along with the bottle of creamer and then retrieved the coffee pot. I poured each cup and then set the carafe on the bamboo trivet in the center of the table.

"What did you mean that Stephen hadn't told Stella everything?" Alec asked when I sat down.

"Maren worked with Dad, and she fell in love with him. It was unrequited because he was fully in love and devoted to Mom."

"I remember now. Maren let it slip the day she showed you a box of your father's things," Alec said.

"If Mom finds that out, then she will treat Maren differently. She should never know about Maren's feelings for him."

"That's right," Kyle said. "Maren still refers to him as Gerry. One of us needs to tell her that she can't say that anymore. Stella will notice that."

I nodded. I liked Maren, but when I had found out her secret feelings for my father, I had lost it. I could only imagine what my mother might do. "I'll talk to her before she sees Mom."

Kyle picked up his phone again. "They're still coming. I guess that Malus Navis has had run-ins with this demon for hundreds of years, if not a thousand years."

"How old is Malus Navis? When was it formed?" Alec asked, taking a sip of his coffee.

"At least a thousand years ago," Kyle answered. "I'm hoping these records will show us how many Seers and Protectors have confronted Jai-ish and how they handled it. Of course, if the Seer and Protector were alone, then there wasn't anyone left to provide the details."

After I took a drink of coffee, I thought about something. "We already break tradition because we don't rely on sacred objects or Latin. Maybe that will be to our advantage."

Kyle nodded, his mind far away. "Maybe."

"After the download is complete, we can print it out. The printer is in my bedroom. It's wireless," Alec said.

"That would be the easiest thing to do. Then we can all look over the entries. Wonder when Stephen can join us?" Kyle asked.

I shrugged. "I don't know. It didn't look like he was getting very far when I left. Do you want me to text him?"

"Just let him know that we all came here," Alec said. "If he can join us, I'm sure he will."

I texted Stephen while we waited for the last document. Finally, Kyle announced the download was complete. He pulled up Alec's wireless printer on his Bluetooth and sent the gigantic file.

"Let's make sure it has paper in it," Alec said and laughed.

I'd never been inside Alec's bedroom before – I'd only seen his bed from the doorway. An antique dresser leaned against the wall to the right of the door with the neatly made king-size bed in the middle of the room. A desk set at the far wall housing Alec's laptop and a large printer. I eased onto the bed while Alec checked the paper tray.

Kyle glanced over at me and raised an eyebrow.

"What?"

"Nothing. I just never thought I'd find myself in Detective Graham's bedroom."

I laughed. "Well, you are pretty."

Alec snorted. "Not *that* pretty."

# CHAPTER SEVEN

Alec, Kyle, and I sat in the living room, studying the entries from the organization that Alec had printed out about Jai-ish. So far, it did not look good. Alec sat on one end of the couch with Kyle on the other end. I sat cross-legged on the floor on the far side of the coffee table.

"Well, I think trying to use blessed objects and speaking Latin is a no-go," Kyle said, sounding exasperated.

"Yes, we kind of already guessed that. That was their tradition," I said, my eyes burning from reading and rereading passages. I tapped the papers in front of me. "In this stack, Jai-ish has killed nine powerful Seers."

"So far, I'm up to seven," Alec said.

"Fourteen," Kyle muttered before taking a long drink from his water bottle. "He only targets the Seers who defeat demon clusters or higher-level demons."

"Which is why he could 'see' them. It's like a moth to a flame." I swallowed. In my own brief history with the Muladach and Malus Navis, I had expelled dozens of demons with only the power of God and my Protector. Jai-ish had seen me.

The doorbell rang, and Alec glanced at us before he stood. "We'll figure it out," he said, sensing my apprehension.

My mouth dropped open when Stephen *and my mother* stepped into the living room.

"Hey, looks like you were able to get the files." Stephen observed the stacks of paper on the coffee table, couch, and floor.

"Maren sent them over," Kyle said. We all stared at Mom, trying to figure out where she fit into this now.

"It's okay," Mom said as she rolled her eyes. "I'm not a ticking time bomb. Hopefully, you all have told me everything. This, um, situation, affects my family, so I'm here to help any way I can." She looked down at me.

I smiled. "Okay, well, these are the files from the archives with any mention of General Jai-ish. Some are very detailed; others are vague. We are trying to narrow it down to see what did and didn't work."

"Correction. What didn't work. Nothing has worked so far," Kyle interjected.

Stephen took a stack of papers, and he and Mom sat down near me on the floor to analyze the files. By late afternoon, we had gotten nowhere. We still weren't any closer to figuring out how to beat Jai-ish except with how I'd defeated the demon cluster in South Carolina.

Alec ordered Chinese food for delivery for a late lunch, and when it arrived, Mom and I took everything into the kitchen to lay it out with plates and forks.

"Alec has a nice home. I'm not sure what I expected," she said, opening a container of General Tso's chicken.

"He's proud of it."

Mom popped a Sweet and Sour Pork bite into her mouth as she studied me moving about the kitchen. Finally, she asked, "You seem very familiar with it. Are you sure this is the first time you've been back here in four years?"

"Yes, I am very sure," I said, taking a glass down from one of the cabinets. "I just have a sharp memory, and Alec hasn't changed anything. How are you and Stephen?"

"Subtle change in subject. I'll allow it." She lowered her voice. "All of this is incredible. If I hadn't heard it from all of you, I would have thought he'd lost his mind. I am angry with your father, though. Angry that I can't yell at him for keeping a secret from me. But I will have to learn to let that go. Stephen is here, and I do love him so much. He's a good man, and I know he loves you and Ben."

I nodded. "He does, Mom. He's always been there for us for anything. Not just for our family, but Kyle and Alec too. When Alec first came to Christ, Stephen was the only person he could talk to because he didn't know any other Christians. He connected Alec to a church in Charlotte where he could make friends and grow. Stephen is selfless. He's the one who wanted you to be told right away about this new threat. He won't keep secrets from you."

"Good." She straightened. "Let's move this food to the dining table so that everyone can serve themselves. I want to get home before Ben. I need to keep a closer eye on him with this demon lurking around. I just wish I could see it."

"No, you don't," I whispered when she'd left the kitchen.

~ ~ ~

Mom drove Stephen, Kyle, and me back to the house about an hour before an ear-bud-wearing Ben arrived. It was strange – Mom bouncing around making Lemon Cream Chicken and sides in the kitchen, Stephen catching up on emails from his church at the dining room table, and Kyle and Ben moving the Xbox into the living room so that they could play a game Ben borrowed from Gavin.

I sat in the nook of the couch pretending to read a book while watching them all. How was I going to protect any of them? If Jai-ish showed up right now, even with my Protector in the same house, I wasn't sure I was strong enough to face him. Plus, I would only have one shot.

I narrowed my eyes at the family portrait on the wall, specifically of Dad. *So, what now? What would you have done if Jai-ish had seen you? And why didn't he see you? Everyone in Malus Navis, including Father Mahon, one of the most respected leaders, said you were the BEST. Why couldn't Jai-ish see you?*

"Hey, Stephen? Can you come downstairs for a second?"

"Yeah. What do you need help with?" he asked without looking up from the laptop.

"I have a question for my Capstone project. It's about how certain children shine like a flare in the night sky. Yet, some educators can't see them."

When Stephen twisted in his chair and looked at me, confusion etched across his face, I stood and motioned for him to come downstairs. Ben had his back to me, concentrating on his game with Kyle.

"I thought you might have some experience with children who shine brightly," I urged.

He blinked. Wow, he wasn't taking the hint.

"Maybe I could offer you some insight on the topic," Mom said. "After all, the members of my family have always been like shining stars, drawing a lot of attention." She emerged from the kitchen headed for the stairs. She threw Stephen a look. At least, she figured it out.

Stephen mumbled something that sounded like *oh, sure*, and followed us to Mom's office where we could shut the door for privacy. Mom patted Stephen's chest when I closed the door after making sure Ben wasn't bounding down the stairs after us.

"A little slow, are we?" she teased.

"I wasn't expecting code phrases. What's on your mind, Ainsley?"

"Dad."

Stephen and Mom exchanged looks.

"Honey, if this is about the engagement-"

"No. No, I'm fine with that. I believe Dad would be fine with it. This is about Dad being the best Seer the organization had had in years and Jai-ish not seeing him. He never targeted Dad. Why?"

Stephen frowned as he sank into Mom's computer chair. "Gerald always wore his medallion."

"We've already surmised that blessed objects won't work," Mom said, unconsciously running her hand over the back of Stephen's neck.

"We need to figure out what Gerald did that was different. I'll try to remember each one of our cases together. Maybe call Maren and see if she can think of anything."

"I'll call Maren. I need to talk to her anyway," I said. "I'll try to get Kyle alone later too. He worked with Dad as a teen, and he might remember something."

I climbed the stairs and went straight to my bedroom, shutting the door behind me. I pulled Maren up on my cell and pressed the icon.

"Ainsley? Hi!"

"Hi, Maren. How are you?"

"Busy. I'm sorry I haven't been around. The school has me teaching Psych during the day, offering counseling sessions in the afternoons and evenings, *and* teaching a virtual class. Did Kyle get those files?"

"Yes, thank you. I have a question for you, and I wanted to mention something else."

"What is it?"

"Mom is helping us now that she knows everything, but I don't want her to ever know how you felt about my father. I know he never cheated on her; however, Mom won't look at you the same way again."

"Of course, I understand."

"Great, thank you. Now to ask you a question. Dad was considered the best within the organization, right?"

"Yes."

"They only brought him in for the most dangerous of demonic cases?"

"Yes, and only if it was a last-ditch effort. He didn't want pulled away from his family unless it was terrible."

"So, when he defeated a demon or a demon cluster, his soul must have shone like a beacon in the other realm. I mean, that's my understanding of what happens when we expel the Muladach."

"That's right. He, um, you, are always takin' a chance of being attacked by more demons right after a banishment."

"Then why didn't Jai-ish come after Dad? Why couldn't he see Dad?"

Maren was silent.

"We think that Dad was doing something that kept him hidden from Jai-ish's view, but we know it wasn't a sacred object. They don't work with Jai-ish. Stephen is trying to remember previous cases with Dad, anything that stuck out to him."

"Does Kyle remember anything?"

"I haven't talked to him about it yet. He's keeping Ben busy."

"Well, I'll think about it, but other than Gerry's necklace, I don't remember anything that would've set him apart from other Seers in how he performed a banishment. He knew Latin and memorized the passages, but as we've seen, *you* can expel a demon cluster while just commanding them to leave in English. Maybe it's not so much what made Gerry invisible, but what's making you outshine all the others."

I closed my eyes. Her answer seemed to make the question that much larger…and impossible. "I'll try to figure it out. Thanks, Maren, Oh, and Maren?"

"Yes?"

"Maybe stop using the term *Gerry*?"

"Sure, Ainsley. Sure," she answered softly.

# CHAPTER EIGHT

"So, Maren thinks that Jai-ish targeting you has more to do with your abilities than with your father's or the other Seers?" Kyle asked as we stood outside my house. Gavin had shown up unannounced, and he and Ben promptly took over the living room. Dinner was in the oven, so I motioned for Kyle to join me outside in the front yard.

"Unless you have another theory." I took in the view from my little hilltop street of the road below. Not many cars passed even on this warmer December evening. My mind raced back to the girl I'd seen the other day, walking quickly to an unknown destination. Again, I couldn't shake the troubling feeling.

Kyle looked down at his sneakers, quiet for a few minutes. Suddenly, he jerked his head up. "You know what I didn't see while we were pouring over those files from the archives?"

I shook my head.

"A duplicate name."

"I'm not sure I follow."

Kyle took a deep breath. "None of the Seers shared the same last name. None of them were related."

"That we know of, I mean, a female Seer could have taken her husband's name."

"Maybe, but as detailed as the archives are, I think the records would mention that. They would read that the Seer was the daughter of so-and-so."

"So, we need to run a check against the database for any Seers whose gift ran in their family," I said, connecting the dots.

"Correct," Kyle agreed as he smiled. "But if I'm right, what sets you apart is that your abilities are multiplied because of your family." He held up his fingers as he counted. "Your power, your father's power, and now Ben's."

"We don't know if Ben-"

"Of course he is. You do know it. According to your father's journal, he knew you were a Seer at fifteen when you saw the lady next door."

"Who had been dead for five months," I whispered, involuntarily glancing up at the picture window of the house beside mine. I hadn't seen the old woman for years now. "Let's pull Mom and Stephen over and tell them what you think. Just don't mention Ben."

"Why?"

"He's thirteen, Kyle. I don't want him involved in this."

"Do you think Jai-ish is going to attack, but then stop and say, 'Oh, wait, this kid is only thirteen! I'd better wait a decade?'" Kyle said in a deep and demonic voice before throwing me a sarcastic look.

I sighed, a bit defeated, knowing what we needed to do. "All right. But we tell them away from Ben."

~ ~ ~

After meeting with Stephen and Mom in the family room and confirming Kyle's theory as plausible, the whole family, including Gavin, ate dinner at the dining room table. It was the first time in years that I'd seen every chair at our dining room table filled. It was a nice feeling.

"When are you guys going to put up your tree?" Gavin asked.

"I don't like it up until about a week before Christmas," Mom answered. "I'm a bit obsessive-compulsive. It bothers me when things are out of place, and to put up decorations means everything isn't where it belongs."

Gavin nodded, and Stephen's eyes grew wide. Surely, he knew that was why our tree was never up until December 17th. I laughed.

Mom narrowed her eyes at me, a playful smile on her lips. "And what is so funny, Ainsley?"

"That you think you are only a *bit* obsessive-compulsive," I remarked, sticking my tongue out at her.

Mom smiled back ruefully. "Careful, Ainsley. Or, you'll find yourself back in your dorm room looking for Santa."

"Do you still have the same room at school?" Kyle asked. He'd visited me once right after I'd moved in. It had been tough to talk with him that weekend because girls I had never met kept stopping by to flirt with him.

"Not the one from Freshman year, but I've had the same one the last three years."

"How do you keep it during summer breaks if you're not at school? When I went in Cali, I always had a new dorm room until I could afford my own apartment."

Mom waved her chicken-loaded fork in the air. "It's a funny story. Ainsley was called into the Financial Aid office at the beginning of her Freshman year, only to be told that Gerald's GI bill wasn't covering everything she needed. We thought she was going to have to quit and come back to it. She called me so upset, and we prayed about it. A couple of days later, she was called back in and told everything was paid for – for the next four years – including her dorm room. A single, no less."

Kyle leaned back in his chair stunned. "Wow. Really? You never told me that," he said to me.

I shrugged as I watched him carefully. "I don't know what to say. I still don't know who paid the balance or why they paid it to make sure I could finish my degree without worrying about funds."

Kyle shook his head, then reached for his fork again. "That's crazy. I mean, I only know one person with that much disposable money who would be willing to cover four years of college expenses."

Everyone at the table got quiet as Kyle thoughtfully chewed his bite of chicken. Finally, Stephen broke the silence.

"Are you saying you paid for Ainsley's school? What the GI bill couldn't cover?"

"Me?" Kyle shook his head. "No. As much as I love you, Reynolds, that's a crapload of money upfront. I'm referring to your Detective Graham."

Mom leaned forward. "You think Alec paid it? How could he afford it?"

Kyle looked over at me, and I dropped my open-mouthed face toward the table. I'd never mentioned to my mother about Alec's finances or his family. It wasn't a secret – it had just never felt right to talk about his personal business.

I took a deep breath before looking straight ahead at Mom. "Alec comes from old money. His grandfather and great-grandfathers were surgeons, but they also founded and invested in several flourishing companies. However, Alec chose to join the Marines and then later become a police officer and finally a detective. He doesn't rely on his trust fund, but it is there. I've always wondered if he was the one who paid for my schooling, but I don't have the guts to ask him. Especially since we hadn't spoken in years until the night before last. I didn't say anything to Kyle about it because he has always thought Alec had an agenda." I looked pointedly at Kyle. "Which he does not."

"If he did have an agenda, he wouldn't have waited four years to tell you. And technically, he still hasn't said anything to you about it." Stephen took a drink of his water, making his point clear to everyone at the table. Alec Graham didn't want or need anything from me.

Gavin nodded his head in my direction with a solemn expression on his young teen face. "I think you should introduce me to this trust-fund friend of yours."

Ben elbowed him, and hysterical laughter exploded all around the table.

~ ~ ~

The next morning at around 6am, Mom peeked her head into my room. "Hey, do you want to join us at the gym?"

"It's 6am, Mom."

"Believe me, I know." Mom walked into my room to look at herself in my dresser mirror. She wore gray leggings, a matching sports bra, and a blue tee tied into a front knot.

"You look cute," I said, slowly sitting up in bed.

"Thanks." She turned to face me. "Stephen and Kyle are coming with me. Ben is already up and dressed. If you want to go, then you need to get moving. We're taking my car."

"Yes, I'll go," I said, willing my body out of bed. "I need to go after all the steak and home-cooked meals."

Mom gave me a quick kiss on the top of my head before she bounded out of my room. "Henry's wife is teaching a Pilates class at 7 o'clock, so hurry!"

I'd personally fallen in love with all things at the gym, but Pilates and yoga were probably my favorites – aside from kickboxing. Henry's wife, Maria, was an incredible instructor and certified in several variations of each. She was patient and sweet, much like her adorable husband, who I'd almost worked for before the events at Queens University and in South Carolina four years ago. Henry was Alec's best friend, and it hadn't seemed right to work with him after that.

I quickly braided my hair and then wrapped it into a bun, washed and moisturized my face with a tinted moisturizer, brushed on some powder, and applied a colored lip balm. I pulled on a pair of royal purple leggings, a sports bra, and a fitted tee with the words *I'd rather coffee* on the front.

I was just putting on my shoes when Kyle knocked on my door. "Are you decent, Reynolds?"

"Would it matter?" I answered when he opened the door without hearing my response first.

"Grumpiness. I like it. Your mother wants you to come on." Kyle was wearing shorts and a muscle tee with his show's logo printed on the front.

"Yes, but when we get back, I'm the first one to the Keurig," I growled as I took the bottle of water he offered and stomped out of the room.

~ ~ ~

By 9am, I was exhausted but happy. I'd taken Maria's hour-long Pilates class and then joined Ben, Kyle, and Stephen in the weight room to work on my upper body. Afterward, when my core and arms felt like jelly, Mom talked me into some time on the elliptical.

Since we lived so close to the gym, none of us had brought clothes to change into, so I went to the locker room to at least splash cold water on myself before I had to pile into Mom's car with four other sweaty people. I vowed to drive my car next time.

When I returned to the gym floor to gather my family to head home, I saw Stephen speaking with a very familiar man. I tucked the loose strands of hair from my bun behind my ears and made myself casually walk across the large room to join Stephen.

"Rafe," Stephen said, motioning for me to come closer when he spotted me. "This is my soon-to-be stepdaughter, Ainsley."

The man smiled at me with his perfect face, but it had somehow lost its allure over the last few days. Probably because Alec and I were on again. Rafe wore workout clothes, shorts and a muscle tee, but he must have just arrived as there wasn't a drop of sweat on him anywhere.

"Yes. Miss Reynolds and I met the other evening at the restaurant. How have you been?"

"Good. Have you been a member long? I haven't seen you here before."

"It is the only gym in Locklyn. When I have had enough of my home gym, I come here for variety."

I couldn't keep from thinking that what I had once thought were the most gorgeous dark blue eyes were actually a bit unsettling. Perhaps because he was so much taller than me, but for a second – maybe for a fraction of a second – I felt fear.

I took a step backward to shake the feeling mentally. The emotion was irrational. Rafe Kae was not going to do anything to me. Plus, I was surrounded by my friends and family. My Protector stood not twenty feet from me, wiping his face with a towel.

"We should get going," I said to Stephen, managing a smile.

"You're right. It is getting a little late in the morning. It was good seein' you again, Rafe."

"You as well, Stephen. I hope to set my eyes on you again, Miss Reynolds," he called after me, but I was already walking to the door, the sensation of dread following me.

Once we were all in the car, I tried to push my thoughts elsewhere. Later in the shower, my mind jumped to reliving that moment, the moment where I felt a tremor of fear. I turned off the water and took a deep breath. It felt like my throat was tightening as if I couldn't swallow. I got out of the shower and brushed my teeth, forcing the sensation to leave.

I'd had enough classes in psychology and health to know that I was in the middle of a panic attack. I stared at my reflection in the mirror. All this talk about Jai-ish and the inevitable defeat of the Seers who confronted him must have made its way into my subconscious. My body was reacting to what could happen even if I wasn't ready to face the truth. I took another deep breath.

I could beat Jai-ish. I just needed to figure out how to do it.

I dressed in a pair of black yoga pants, a navy blue fitted tee, and a pair of navy blue ankle socks with tiny pineapples on them. I studied my reflection as I wrapped my still damp hair up into a bun. I'd gained control of my breathing again, but I needed to remind myself to breathe deeply and keep my mind occupied elsewhere.

I found a slightly damp from the shower Kyle leaning against the counter drinking a cup of coffee in the kitchen. "You've been quiet since we left the gym," he observed.

I closed the Keurig machine on the pod of jelly donut flavored coffee and chose the large size. As it whirred to life, I pulled a skillet from a lower cabinet and a carton of eggs from the refrigerator.

"I think my mind is trying to cope with this threat from Jai-ish. I'm pretty sure I had a panic attack in the shower."

Kyle set his cup down and grabbed my shoulders, forcing me to face him. "We are going to work this out. You have an entire team of people all over the country searching the database for you. You have your mom and your brother, Stephen, Graham, and, of course, the devastatingly handsome me."

I let out a small laugh. "Well, that makes me feel better."

"Good. Why don't you go watch TV or something, and I'll make breakfast for everyone?"

"Are you sure?"

"Yes, I know how to cook, Reynolds."

I thanked Kyle, grabbed my coffee, and headed into the living room. *A Christmas Story* was on cable, and I settled in to watch it. However, within minutes the doorbell rang.

"I'll get it," I yelled. I wasn't sure where Mom and Stephen were, but there was no reason to disturb them.

Alec stood on the front porch, dressed in his off-hours attire of jeans and leather jacket.

"Hey," he said as he stepped into the foyer and kissed me. "I'm off work today, so I thought I would swing by and get an update."

"Ben's in his room," I whispered. "He gets three weeks off for Christmas due to year-round school. Come on up. *Kyle* is making breakfast."

"Don't lie," Alec teased, shedding his jacket and hanging it up on the hook behind the front door, revealing a gray thermal henley.

I walked up the stairs to the living room with Alec following. "What exactly is the punishment for lying to a detective?" I asked in my most sultry voice.

"I can hear you!" Kyle's voice came from the kitchen. "You're making me want to vomit. Go, watch TV! Graham, come in here for a second."

I made a face at Alec before resuming my place on the couch. Alec followed the voice into the kitchen.

It was a little while before Mom plopped down beside me. "So Kyle and Alec are making breakfast? Weird."

"I know. Wonder what they're up to?"

"Who knows? Stephen just joined them."

"Trouble, if you ask me."

"Why are you talking about me? I leave you for five minutes…" Stephen emerged from the kitchen with a cup of coffee in his hand.

"Just feeling a little outnumbered, Stephen dear." Mom smiled up at him.

I moved over so Stephen could join us for the movie. It wasn't long before breakfast was ready and on the table. Eggs, bacon, biscuits, and gravy. All the good things.

After we ate, we started back into the living room to find a new movie to watch when Alec made the most exciting and startling announcement.

"Stella, if it's all right with you and Stephen, I would like to take Ainsley on a weekend trip."

"Sounds good to me," Stephen said immediately with a smile and a nod.

Mom, however, raised an eyebrow. "A weekend away? Alone?"

"Separate rooms, I promise." Alec gave her his charming grin – the one that always melted me into a puddle on the floor.

"I think it sounds great," Kyle piped in while sitting on the couch with his legs stretched out. "Some time away from all the chaos and stress. If you were my kid, I'd say yes."

"Well, now, if *Kyle* agrees," Mom groaned, throwing her hands in the air.

"I'm safer with Alec than just about anyone," I said.

Kyle snorted, but when we looked at him, he just waved his hand for us to ignore him. Apparently, he couldn't contain his honest thoughts about Alec inside *all* the time. Bless him.

Mom studied me for a moment. I didn't have to remind her that I was twenty-two years old and a senior in college. She was just her usual worried mother self.

"Okay, but please be careful. Alec, where is it you want to take her?"

"It's a secret."

"Excuse me?" Both of her eyebrows shot up.

Alec put a hand up as if shielding himself from Stella's soon to come physical impact. "Not a secret from you. From her. I'll tell you when she's out of the room."

"Oh, good," Mom said, smiling. "Ainsley, go to your room and pack, so Alec and I can talk."

~ ~ ~

"Where are we going?"

"I'm taking you someplace I love," Alec answered as he drove the truck down the middle lane of the interstate.

"But why did you tell me to pack a weekend bag?"

"Because we are staying in a cabin."

When I didn't answer him, Alec glanced in my direction. "You can stop hyperventilating over there. It has two bedrooms downstairs and a loft upstairs. Separate rooms, just like I told Stella."

"I'm not hyperventilating. You act like I haven't stayed in a hotel with you before."

"We had separate rooms then, too, if you remember."

"I remember. I remember wishing that we weren't in separate rooms - minus Stephen, of course. But, I was young and naive. I had a fantasy in my head of the way I thought we should be. That didn't work out."

"Are you ever going to forgive me?" he asked, staring at the road.

"I did forgive you. It still bothers me. You didn't even try to fight for us. I turned eighteen only six weeks later."

"Ainsley, there was more to it than that. I had some things to work out for myself. Baggage I didn't want to haul into a relationship with you. Plus, I thought moving out of the way would give you a chance to experience life on your own, meet new people, and do things."

"You could've lost me forever. I dated a guy for a little while in college."

"Are you talking about the guy who got pulled over for dead tags and no driver's license on his third offense?"

My mouth dropped open. "Were you checking up on me?"

Alec grinned as he stared out at the interstate. "I just wanted to make sure he was worth your time."

"That wasn't your decision to make."

"So, I was wrong?"

"Well…no. He had some issues. We broke up anyway. He didn't pass Mom's approval."

Alec laughed. "Stella seems happy."

"Yes. She's in love. She and Stephen are cute together. Plus, Ben likes having Stephen come down and visit. Whether Stephen knows it or not, he's filling the father role that Ben desperately needs now that he's a teenager."

"How do you feel about it?"

"About Stephen? I love him. He's great. I think Dad chose well."

"What do you mean?"

I swept my hair up into a bun as I remembered the visitation from my father. "Four years ago, Mom had a dream about Dad, but I think it was a visitation because I'd had one from him too when we were at Ashbury. He convinced Mom to call his friend Stephen about attending a church. Mom said the dream was so real that she called Stephen. After she told him about it, he drove down that night from West Virginia and arrived in the morning. You should have seen his face when we went to dinner that evening. He took one look at Mom all dressed up, and I swear, I think he fell in love with her right then."

Alec was glancing back and forth from me to the road with a grin on his face. "I love it when you talk about your family. Your whole face lights up."

"I love them. Speaking of family, how is your grandfather Edward?"

"He passed away about a year ago."

"Oh, I'm so sorry." Although Edward wasn't a fan of mine, he was Alec's only blood relative that I'd met.

"I told Tilda to stay in the house, and I go down and visit as often as I can. You're not going to believe this, but I got Tilda to attend a church service with me in Hilton Head last year. She got saved at the age of seventy. Since I inherited my grandfather's estate, I hired a caretaker, so Tilda can spend the rest of her life relaxing. She deserves it. She helped raise my dad and me. She was the only good thing about living there."

I pressed my lips together as I reached for Alec's hand. "That's great news. I always liked Tilda. She visited me at the hotel in South Carolina when we were investigating the Ashbury Estate."

"I didn't know that," he answered as he rubbed his thumb over my hand. "Why?"

"She wanted to know if I was pregnant."

"Good Lawd! I'm glad you never told me. Did you tell her we couldn't even date back then?"

"Yes. I think I laughed at the irony." I let the moment elongate into silence as Alec drove, and I remembered my conversation with Tilda about Alec's anger. "Are you taking me wherever you are taking me because you want us to have a fresh start? I mean, us kissing again, does that mean you want something serious?"

"Do you want something serious?"

"I want to know what your intentions are."

"As I told you, I'm taking you someplace that I love. I want to share it with you. It's a place I've visited several times in the past few years. Except, every time I was there, I could only think about what your reaction would be to see it."

"How long before we get there?"

Alec took an exit ramp and slowed down at a stop sign. He squeezed my hand. "It takes about eight hours." When my eyes grew wide, Alec added, "I also want to spend time with you without Kyle, or Stephen, or the Locklyn Police Department, or demons always in the forefront. My goal by the end of the weekend is to make you fall in love with me."

My heart fluttered as I smiled at Alec. He had no idea that I'd fallen head over heels in love with Detective Alec Graham four years ago, the first time I'd run my hand over the stubble on his face.

~ ~ ~

We'd left Locklyn at around 12:30pm, stopped for a fast-food drive-thru dinner at five, and arrived at Smoke Hole Resorts at Seneca Rocks in West Virginia at a little after eight. Alec had driven to the gift shop, a large log building with a red metal roof and an attached lodge, to pick up the key from the owner before they closed.

When he got back into the truck, I asked, "So, we're not staying at the lodge? There's a cabin nearby?" It was already pretty dark out.

"Yup, just a few miles down the road. They have several family and honeymoon cabins."

"Honeymoon cabins?" I leaned toward him in the truck and wrapped my fingers around his wrist. "I thought you said separate rooms?"

"I did." Smiling, he playfully pushed me away. "I can't be alone with you in a honeymoon cabin. That would require too much restraint on my part."

I laughed until we turned into the drive of a neat semi-circle of cabins. The smaller ones, which I assumed were the honeymoon cabins, were identical with wooden front porches that held a swing and two windows facing the small parking spot.

"They look like tiny houses."

Alec made a right turn away from the smaller cabins to a row of what had to be the family cabins. These were identical; log cabins with large front porches, a swing, a picnic table on the little grassy area near the parking spot, and two windows facing the front.

Within ten minutes, Alec had us settled inside with a fire started in the stone fireplace. The inside was even nicer than the exterior. The living room looked like something out of a magazine with rich plaid furniture, cushions, blankets, flat-screen television on the wall, and lamps that shone neither too bright nor too dim.

The kitchen had everything; a refrigerator, stove, microwave, coffeemaker, plates, utensils, and cookware with a table and four chairs in front of the window. Near the kitchen was the small bathroom, and next to that was our bedrooms – right next door to one another. My bedroom had a lovely oak headboard, nightstands, and a dresser. Wooden stairs led from the living room to the loft. If I had been staying with Mom and Ben, I was pretty sure I would have fought Ben for the loft. The single twin-size bed and dresser with the A-frame ceiling were too cozy to pass up.

"This place is gorgeous," I said, kneeling beside Alec as he stoked the fire with the poker. The scent from the logs and the crackling sound made the evening magical.

"Wait until you see it in the daytime. The view of the rocks from the back porch is glorious. There is a pond we can walk to sometime."

"What is that large building with all the windows across from us?"

"It's a venue used for conferences, weddings, and such."

"How convenient."

Alec smiled. "Wow, you are a jumper, aren't you? First, you want a honeymoon cabin, and now a wedding venue."

I interlocked my arm in his free one and leaned into him. "Honestly, I'm just happy to be here with you."

He kissed me softly on the lips before resuming his work on the fire. "You needed a break. Kyle told me about the panic attack."

I stiffened. "Kyle told you? Why?"

"He's worried about you. He wouldn't have told me otherwise."

"So…is that why you invited me here? Is that why Stephen and Kyle practically shoved me out the door?" I asked, pushing myself up to stand. I walked into the kitchen and opened the refrigerator. Alec had purchased a few groceries with us, including a case of bottled water. I grabbed a bottle, unscrewed the lid, and took a long drink. When I shut the fridge door, Alec was standing there.

He took the bottle from my hand and set it on the table behind me. "I invited you here to make you fall in love with me *and* to get your mind off this threat." He encircled my waist with his hands and pulled me closer. "I do intend to make good on that promise."

Alec kissed me, but just as I was withering under his spell, he pulled away. "I've got games in the SUV. I'll go out and get them."

"Games? Like Twister?" I asked, peering up at him through my lashes.

Alec stopped at the door and turned to look at me. "You're so bad," he said, with a fake look of shock on his face.

~  ~  ~

The following day, I awoke with the sunlight streaming through the bedroom window. I smiled. Alec and I had stayed up all night, *not* making out but talking and laughing and playing the most ridiculous board games. He must have bought every game Walmart sold when he ran in for our groceries. If my friends Molly or Freya would've asked me a few years ago what I would have done with Alec if left alone for a weekend, it wouldn't have been to play board games.

But Alec and I both had grown over the last four years. I'd grown into an adult, and both of us had grown as Christians. It felt good to be with him, comfortable. We had passion, and sometimes that was hard to contain, but we also had an easy, laid-back relationship that seemed to make everything click.

I quickly dressed in jeans, a hoodie, socks, and a pair of slip-on boots. I snuck into the bathroom but heard Alec moving around in the kitchen. Hopefully, he was making breakfast. I was starving. When I finished, I went back into the bedroom, grabbed my Bible for morning devotion, and made the bed before joining Alec.

"Good morning, beautiful," he said as he gave me a sweet kiss on the lips before shoving a massive mug of coffee at me. "Take this. You're going to need it."

"Why?"

"Follow me."

I followed him to the back door, and when he opened it, I held my breath. The back porch was relatively small, but it overlooked a creek that ran by the cabins. The view of the rocks on the mountain was beautiful. A layer of frost decorated the field, separating us from the surrounding hills. We sat down on the two rocking chairs on the porch to admire the view with our mugs of coffee.

"I didn't know that anything like this existed."

"You haven't seen the world yet, Ainsley. When I would come up to West Virginia to visit Stephen, I'd always make a detour to Seneca Rocks, rent a cabin, and stay for a few days. I'd come out here in the morning to look at the view and then again at night to take in the stars."

"Can we do that tonight?"

"Sure. We'll bring a couple of the blankets out here to wrap up in."

"And make hot cocoa."

Alec laughed. "Hot cocoa, it is. We can go out later today and find some. I bet the gift shop has it. You might want some souvenirs, too."

When I started to protest about the cost, Alec added, "My treat, I insist."

We sat in silence, looking up at the rock formations, drinking coffee, and holding hands. *God, if this is the one truly happy moment with Alec, I'll live to see, then thank you. Don't ever let me forget this time with him.*

A sudden sensation filled my chest. I would do anything to relive this moment. Face anything to spend the rest of my life with Alec. I would fight for us. Not only would I fight for my family, I would fight Jai-ish for my future.

~ ~ ~

Smoke Hole Resort not only featured a fantastic gift shop, but they offered tours of the underground caverns. Unfortunately, it was winter, and the caverns were closed. Alec and I picked up some souvenirs for our friends and family, hot cocoa, mugs with *Seneca Rocks, WV* printed on the front, and different types of homemade candy. The shop also sold clothing and blankets, so I picked up a shawl for Molly, a scarf for Freya, who was still at the University of South Carolina, and a quilt for my bed.

Alec took our haul back to the cabin, dropped them in the living room, and then we took off to walk around the area. We stopped at the small pond and fed the koi. Thankfully, it wasn't quite cold enough for the water to freeze completely yet. This December was unusually warm in West Virginia, to hear Alec tell it.

We baked a frozen lasagna in the oven for dinner and then made smores at our fireplace. It was the loveliest and coziest weekend I had ever spent with someone.

"I want to come back next year," I said as I leaned into Alec's arm in front of the fire.

"Maybe a little earlier in the year. You do not want to drive on these hills when they're iced up." His Southern roots slipped for a second when he said the word *iced*, and I stifled a laugh.

"What?"

"Your accent. Sometimes it slips out. Just on certain words."

Alec leaned down and cupped my chin in his hand. "Well, as long as you understand me." He gave me a long, slow kiss that left me feeling overheated in my hoodie.

His cell rang before I had a chance to remark about changing my clothes. "You have cell reception now?"

Alec jumped up and swooped his phone up from the table. "Barely." He walked around the cabin, trying to answer the call. Apparently, the caller couldn't hear him. He took the phone outside to the front porch.

I hugged my knees to my chest as I sat on the floor, the crackling from the fire relaxing me even more.

Alec came back inside and locked the door behind him. "That was Stephen. I'll call him from the truck after we get on the road in the morning."

"Did he say what he wanted? Is everyone okay?"

"Everyone is fine. It was hard to make out what he was saying because of the mountains here. Too much interference."

"I could message him on social."

"No," Alec said, pulling me up to my feet. "It's nothing that can't wait until tomorrow. Right now, you and I are going to snuggle up on the back porch with these blankets and watch the stars."

"Hmm, I like that plan, Detective."

# CHAPTER NINE

Alec and I left Seneca Rocks early the next morning after dropping the key off for our cabin in a dropbox outside the gift shop. By leaving at 8am, we hoped to reach Locklyn by 4:00, even if we stopped for a quick lunch. We'd been on the road about an hour when I insisted that we call Stephen.

The preacher answered on the third ring. "Alec, did you two enjoy your weekend?"

Alec and I looked at each other and smiled. "Very much so, Stephen. It's beautiful at Seneca Rocks this time of year. I wish I could have shown Ainsley what it looks like in the Fall."

"Good, good. Stella was worried about Ainsley but didn't want to call and bother you. Alec, did you hear everything I said last night on the phone?"

Alec glanced at me, then back to the road. "Just bits and pieces. I have you on speakerphone."

Stephen hesitated for a moment before continuing, "We found out more on Jai-ish."

"Like what?" I asked.

"Unlike the Muladach you've faced in the past, Jai-ish can not only influence a person or a group of people; he can *possess* a single individual."

"Possess? You mean like The-Exorcist-spewing-green-stuff possession?" That sounded much worse than the Muladach.

"I mean possess as he becomes them, and not a hissing, snarling humanoid either. An intelligent fallen angel inhabiting someone else, taking over their life, and interacting with people."

"Crap," Alec muttered.

"So," I started slowly, trying to nail down the specific details, "Jai-ish is more dangerous than the Muladach because he could be inside anyone? How will we know if he is near? Will I feel something like I do with the other demons? Does he ever attack in his supernatural form?"

"Woah, slow down. We found an entry about a Seer that you can read when you get here. There was a witness from the organization there during the confrontation and goes into great detail."

"Awesome. I mean, not awesome because obviously, Jai-ish killed the Seer, but awesome that we have a detailed account." I pushed my lips together to keep from speaking. What was wrong with me?

"We should be back to Ainsley's house between four and five."

"All right. be careful."

~ ~ ~

I called Mom about an hour out from Locklyn to tell her to order dinner and that Alec and I would pick it up on our way home. I wanted to pour over this new information without worrying about getting dinner started, served, and cleaned up.

It was after six by the time Alec and I had unloaded the truck, and Mom had laid out the turkey and stuffing dinner from our favorite family restaurant like a banquet on the kitchen counter.

I made myself a plate of food and then settled into a chair at the dining table to read over the entry. Alec said he would go over it when I finished.

*Malus Navis Member Eli Keach in regards to Seer Charles Howards Grimm,*

*Date 28 November 1929*

*The demon, known as Jai-ish, sent a message through a woman that the demon who leads hordes of the creatures has seen our Seer Charles Howards Grimm. Grimm handles our cases on the East Coast. We have trusted this gifted Seer with more than two dozen cases over the past decade, and he has successfully banished demons in all of them.*

*This is why that perhaps Jai-ish has decided Grimm is an obstacle for the demonic community. The woman told Grimm that Jai-ish has seen him and that his demise is very soon. The woman convulsed and died shortly thereafter.*

*Grimm behaves as if this threat has no meaning to him. Although the man is gifted, he is arrogant in many ways. It is his great flaw. Thank God for **His** grace because, at times, I do not know about Grimm's soul!*

*Date 30 November 1929*

*The most horrible thing happened today, one of which I knew in the depths of my soul would occur.*

*I had met with Charles Howards Grimm about a case in Roanoke, Virginia. Three school-age boys had gone missing from an exclusive boarding school located within the hills surrounding the city. The administration called upon Father*

Nero to investigate. Since the elder priest is also a Protector, he picked up on the energy from demonic activity and surmised that the boys were still alive although being held captive somewhere near the academy.

It took Grimm and me two days before we could reach The Academy at Narrows for Gifted Boys outside of Roanoke. I accompanied Grimm into the school, where we questioned the administrators and the male teacher. The boys were within the same group in school and taught by the same instructor for many of their studies, a Mister Coffey, with the exception of Latin; a beautiful young woman in her early twenties with dark mahogany brown hair taught foreign languages. Looking back, I did think it was odd that such a young woman would be teaching at a private school for boys. The only other females within the brick former residential mansion were the older cook and the two cleaning ladies - all three way past their prime.

Father Nero joined Grimm and me outside of the school where the Seer and Protector felt the strongest energy waves. The older priest and I followed Grimm towards the woods as he seemed focused on a spot ahead of us, his blessed dagger hanging from his side. Grimm was a force to be reckoned with, a man who was no stranger to boxing and the heavy weights. I had seen him take down opponents, both human and demon alike, although with very different executions and outcomes.

*Through the woods, we came to a clearing with a stone wine cellar built above ground. The wooden doors were large, and from my estimation, I gathered the cellar was most likely close to a hundred fifty years old. Both the Father and Grimm stopped forty yards from the doors.*

*"Do you hear that, Grimm?"*

*"Yes, Father."*

*"What do you hear?" I whispered, silently chiding myself. It is difficult to record work for Malus Navis when I do not possess supernatural abilities like my counterparts.*

*"Children crying," Father Nero answered.*

*"Not children," Grimm said, his face solemn. "Demons mimicking the children."*

*"Does that mean the boys are indeed dead?" I asked.*

*Neither man answered me as they slowly started for the doors. Grimm placed his hand on the door and "listened" in that strange way. Father Nero followed by pressing his palm to the wood, a frown forming above his brow.*

*"Stay back, Eli," Grimm ordered as he motioned me to the side of the building, but I only moved to the corner, out of sight in case whatever was inside looked past Father Nero and Grimm. Grimm pulled one of the heavy doors open with a silent groan, although it was written upon his face. The two men stood looking into the wine cellar. It was then I realized*

*that everything in the clearing was quiet; not even a bird chirped nor a rabbit moved in the brush.*

*The priest nodded at Grimm, permitting him to enter the cellar. Father Nero followed. I waited until the count of three in my head before looking around the corner of the standing door.*

*The two men stood in the extensive cellar, looking down upon the corpses of the three missing boys. I moved into the room with my back against the stone wall so as not to disturb them but close enough to hear their conversation.*

*"We are too late, Grimm," Father Nero said in anguish.*

*Grimm bent down near the head of one of the boys - a dark-haired boy, no older than eight years. He touched the boy's neck. "He is still warm. This has only occurred." He glanced around, searching the room for an invisible enemy. "The kidnapper — correction, the murderer — must have left only moments before we arrived."*

*Father Nero kneeled beside the boys, all in a row, and said his prayers over them. Grimm joined me near the door. "Does anything seem out of sorts to you, Eli?"*

*"I don't hear anything. What I mean is that everything is silent. No birds."*

*Grimm listened and then frowned. "No birds," he mumbled. As he turned to leave the cellar to test our theory on* the lack of sound, suddenly, the female teacher appeared in the doorway.

"Oh, excuse me, gentlemen! I had no idea anyone was here. I saw the doors open and came to shut them. We keep them shut during the-"

The woman's mouth quickly closed as she viewed, where the priest stood, the neatly displayed bodies of her former students. Her eyes grew wide as she stared up in horror at Grimm.

"Please do not be frightened. We only just came upon them ourselves." Father Nero held his hands out to her as if to comfort her, but the woman backed away. Then as if curiosity got the best of the teacher, she came into the wine cellar and moved past Grimm and the priest.

"Miss, you will not want to see them so close. One of the boys has been dead for quite a while," Grimm said.

"Oh, no," the woman said, her voice taking on a hard edge. "It is you who should not see them so close." She turned towards the three of us near the door. Her eyes were ablaze with light as I had never seen before. On my past excursions with Grimm, I had witnessed men influenced by the demons, their eyes reflective of the light around them. But this woman - her eyes shone from a fire **within** her.

I pushed my back against the stone wall as Grimm launched his dagger at the woman. I expected the knife to land in her breast, but she deflected the weapon, and it landed on the stone floor with a clatter. Father Nero and Grimm began to recite an ancient Latin passage in unison. The woman took a step backward but only smiled a devilish grin at the men.

"Is that all you have to offer me this time, Malus Navis? An old priest and a strong man? This is your most powerful Seer and Protector? I have ground the bones of past Seers with only a look. I have flicked my wrist and watched as their eyeballs melted from the sockets. I have whispered to them and blew death into their souls. So, what is this? It is an insult to me."

Throughout this speech, the two men continued to speak Latin until Grimm finally asked, "And who **are** you, woman?"

"Oh, Charles Howards Grimm, I am Jai-ish. I am the one who is to end you."

Grimm's jaw clenched. "Are you the one who murdered these boys? Do you possess this woman?"

The woman took a step forward, a sneer on her face. "Of course. How else was I to lure you here, the Great and Impulsive Grimm? Do you still believe that you cannot be killed?"

Grimm stood motionless as the question hung in the air. Father Nero paused to take a breath.

"And you, Theodore Nero. Just as Grimm's arrogance is his downfall, I see your vice as well."

I stood in terror as both men stopped moving, no longer speaking, as they stared off into space. Why were they not fighting this demon?

The woman turned to me. "Now you, I do not have permission to harm you. I cannot kill you. Not yet. Do not even let me hear of your name, but do observe for Malus Navis. Tell them that the next Seer and Protector I see will suffer a worse fate than these two men."

She turned on her heel, the stiff skirt around her lower half not hindering her at all. She stood in front of Father Nero. "Do you see your sin? The one you continue in?" she seethed in the man's face. She touched his chin. "Yes, there it is. I see it too."

Then with a quick movement, I can only describe as instantaneous, she grabbed Father Nero's arm with both hands and pulled it off! As blood splattered and sputtered on the stone floor, the priest screamed as his brain must have realized what had been done to him. In another second, the woman ripped his head off with both hands, and I watched as my mentor's body hit the floor with a sickening thud.

If I had wanted to scream, I found I could not. The fear and terror seized me. I could not even pray at that moment;

so frightened I was, not only for myself but also for what I anticipated would happen to my friend Charles Grimm.

Grimm still stood, mute and motionless. He had not even so much as flinched while the woman possessed by Jai-ish was murdering Father Nero. The woman moved to stand in front of Grimm now, running her hand up his arm, over his shoulder and neck, and into his hair, tousling like a parent would their unruly child. "And do you see the sin that still ensnares you so easily, Charles Howards Grimm? The one you felt did not matter in the scheme of things? The one you could have stopped and turned from but **chose** not to?" She stood on her toes to reach his ear and whispered loud enough for me to hear. "That is your undoing."

The woman took a step away from Grimm, and with only a flick of her wrist, Grimm let out a small groan, and then I heard horrible noises, bubbling sounds that I, even now, cannot describe. Bits of flesh fell onto the floor near his boot. I would soon find out that the bits of flesh had once been his eyes. Then Grimm fell silent before he dropped onto his knees and pitched forward onto the stone floor. Later, I learned that his healthy heart had suddenly stopped.

The woman gave me a dismissive glance before leaving the wine cellar. "Do not forget to retell everything you have seen here today, boy." With that, she bristled out through the doorway.

*I am ashamed to say that I stayed there in the wine cellar for at least an hour. I could not bring myself to leave the bodies of Father Nero or Grimm. I could not leave the bodies of the three innocent boys who were used as pawns to trap the Seer and Protector. I could not leave because I was afraid that she would be waiting for me in the clearing.*

*But I should not have worried. When Jai-ish had finished with the teacher, he used her body to climb to the school's roof and fall to her death. I never did learn her name. If the school administration mentioned it to me, I was in shock and never heard it.*

*Father Nero, Grimm, and I had only experienced demons outside of the human body, ones who influence people to do evil things. Jai-ish possessed the woman utterly and fully. There was no saving her. There was no saving the priest or Grimm.*

*This will be my final entry for Malus Navis. I have lost two dear friends today in gruesome ways that will haunt me forever. I am detailing this entry for the next powerful pair of Seer and Protector: If you are given the message concerning Jai-ish, know that not only has your light drawn him to you, but he will use your sin against you. Search your heart, repent, and then seal your heart. Do not give him passage. I believe both Father Nero and Grimm were envisioning their past sin, perhaps something they could not end, and that is how Jai-ish got a foothold.*

*Search your heart, Seers. Repent, Protectors. Seal your heart from the enemy. It is with great heaviness in my heart that I say purity is the only way to defeat this enemy. Seers, you are the Beacon. Make your light so undeniably bright that it sends Jai-ish and all of his horde back to Hell.*

*In memory of Father Theodore Nero and Charles Howards Grimm,*

*~Eli Keach~*

"Well? How's it look?" Alec asked from the chair beside me when I set my fork down and blinked. I hadn't noticed, but Kyle sat in the chair across from me. He was staring at me with the most somber expression on his face I had ever seen.

I looked from Kyle to Alec, then placed the palms of my hands over my eyes and leaned on my elbows at the table.

"That bad?" Alec whispered, pulling the stapled papers from under my arms to read for himself.

"Oh, Kyle!" I moaned as I removed my hands and stared into Kyle's serious blue eyes. "We have never faced anything like this before."

Kyle didn't answer, only reached across the table and grabbed my hand.

"What Jai-ish did to them…what Eli saw…where do we even start?" As hard as I tried, I could not keep the hot tears from stinging my eyes. Reading Eli's descriptive words had created images in my mind. Images I couldn't shake, no matter how many times I tried.

Kyle let go of my hand to come around to the other side of the table. He pulled me up with such force and hugged me that I was both stunned and grateful. Kyle was my friend. The Protector to my Seer. He was in this too, and if Eli was to be believed, then it wasn't just me Jai-ish was coming after. Kyle was in just as much danger.

Kyle held me as we stood beside the dining room table until we heard Alec's sharp intake of breath. "What the…" he started to say but trailed off. I knew exactly at what point of the entry he was reading. When Alec finished, he slammed the paper down on the table.

"You are not facing Jai-ish. We can hide you. I have friends in the FBI."

"That won't work, Alec," Stephen said from the recliner at the picture window. He had sat in the chair the entire time, watching us read, and absorb, the horrible details. Details that he could never have told me over the phone. "It won't work because this isn't a human enemy; it's a spiritual one. From what I've been told, the current heads of Malus Navis knew this could happen in our lifetime. After all, *malus navis* is Latin for beacon. Jai-ish can locate her anywhere. *She's* the Beacon."

"But, Stephen, he killed them! Did Jai-ish doom both Father Nero and Charles Grimm to Hell?" I moved to stand in front of him, working to keep the tears from making my voice crack.

Stephen shook his head as he rose, placing his hands on my shoulders. "No! He can't send Christians to Hell. He doesn't have that type of power. Father Nero and Grimm were both Christians saved by grace who just hadn't completely kicked something. I don't know their vices, but I know that they were both marked by Jesus. Jai-ish took their lives using that woman, but he couldn't touch their souls – no matter what he told Eli Keach. Remember what Jesus prayed in the Book of John? Jesus thanked God that not one of those given to Him is lost. We belong to God and to His Son, Jesus – *no one* can snatch us out of His hand. Sin ensnares each one of us, but remember we are more than conquerors through Christ. Right?"

Stephen looked up at Kyle and Alec, who had come to stand behind me. "I suggest we all follow Eli's advice: search our hearts, repent of any wrong and turn away from it, and ask God to seal it to keep it pure."

~ ~ ~

Purity.

I laid in bed thinking about that word. Since becoming a Christian four years ago, I had grown. I studied my Bible, followed a devotional app on my phone, and listened to the word preached on Sundays. I read and reread Jesus' words and learned how He and the disciples sent demons scurrying from the bodies of men.

Okay, so maybe I did flirt with quite a number of guys after I found myself and gained confidence. But I didn't sleep around. I was still a virgin. Although I seriously wondered at times if I would be able to keep to my non-negotiable premarital self-imposed vows when it came to Alec. Jesus had said that if you looked at someone with lust, you had committed adultery in your heart. Lust was a sin, and when it came to Alec....

But, I had managed to spend a weekend with him in a beautiful cabin far away from family and friends and not give in. That had to count for something, right?

I was guilty of lying to my mother in the past, hating spiteful girls, and wishing I had the things that other people did. What was that? Dishonoring my parents, murder in the eyes of God, and covetousness. Three out of the ten commandments. Throw in adultery in my heart, and I was in trouble.

*Lord, forgive me. God, help me not to give in to lust or anything else. You make a way of escape. Come to think of it, You always have. There was that time I was alone with Alec in my house, and the few times we were alone in the hotel room. You always sent someone to interrupt us, allowing us to take a breath and get our common sense back. Please help me with purity. Hide me from Jai-ish. In Jesus' name, Amen.*

My phone dinged.

Alec: **I love you, baby. Good night.**

*God, please let me survive this so I can marry Alec one day.*

Me: **I love you more.**

~ ~ ~

Kyle and I climbed out of his rental car the following evening in front of the police station. Alec had called with news on the late Mark Tahl, the professor of Religious Studies at the University of North Carolina at Chapel Hill, but he thought it would be better to tell us in person.

That didn't bode well.

As Kyle and I walked toward the building, a sudden wave rippled through the air, twisting and manipulating the scenery. My equilibrium began to rise and fall as dizziness and a queasy feeling threatened to make me pass out. I reached for Kyle's arm to steady myself.

"I see it too," he said in a dry voice.

The vibrational energy tremored again, and I choked back vomit. The force twisted, moving behind us and then toward the alley on the other side of the parking lot.

Kyle made a clicking sound with his tongue. "Well, the sane side of me is saying we should not go in there."

A scream suddenly highlighted the night. "We have to go now," I yelled as I took off running toward the scream. Kyle and I both came to the entryway to the alley within seconds, but the screaming had stopped. It was already dark, and this alley didn't have many streetlights. The only light was what shined from the back of random houses, some of it barely lighting the darkness. The scream came again in one short burst.

"There!" Kyle said.

I could barely make out a girl, probably around Ben's age, crouched in front of a closed garage door. She wore jeans and a jacket with a toboggan that had a large puff sewn on at the top, and from the sound of it, she was crying. The girl was familiar.

"Hey," Kyle said softly. "We're not going to harm you. Are you lost? Did someone hurt you?"

I followed Kyle, peering into the backyards. There had to be a reason she had been screaming.

"Right around the corner is the police station. My friend and I could walk you over there."

We were so close to her now that Kyle went down on one knee to meet her at eye level. The girl just stared mutely at us as the sensation of dread filled my belly. I was pretty sure this was the girl I'd seen from my house.

"I'm Kyle, and this is Ainsley. A friend of ours works at the police station. Maybe we can help you. Where do you live?"

The girl began to give a low guttural laugh in response to Kyle's question. At once, he stood, almost knocking me backward.

"You know where I live, boy," the girl said. Except it wasn't the girl. It couldn't have been. Her voice was deep yet icy. That tremor of fear I'd felt last week at the gym returned.

She slowly stood as Kyle and I continued to back away. The voice in my head screamed. *Retreat, Ainsley! For the love of God, run!*

But I didn't, and neither did Kyle.

The girl started walking towards us. "I must say I am impressed at how well you have handled yourselves. Taking down hordes of demons is not easy. I knew the two of you would become a problem."

"Jai-ish?" I didn't recognize my own voice.

The girl tilted her head to the side to look directly at me. "Your father was a problem."

With that, the sensation in my chest grew and twisted from fear to fury. I grabbed Kyle's hand and found my voice. Pointing at the girl, I commanded, "Be gone, demon! You are not permitted to enter this realm, and you cannot harm this girl. Leave, and return to Hell!"

The girl took a step back as she watched us.

Kyle and I walked forward, gaining ground. "You must leave in the name of Jesus Christ. Back to Hell and never return to this girl again!"

She was breathing heavily now, and I silently prayed that the girl who was in there was still alive. She studied us for a moment letting her eyes fall on me again, then brought her palm to her face, kissed it, and then blew on her hand.

Did she just blow me a *kiss*?

I felt a slight breeze and my hair lift a bit from my shoulders. I narrowed my eyes at the girl, but she only raised her chin in defiance.

"I said to leave in the name of Jesus-"

She blew another "kiss" in Kyle's direction, except instead of the breeze passing by him, Kyle let out a surprised scream as he suddenly dropped to one knee.

"Kyle!"

He pushed me away from him when I tried to help him stand. "Finish it, Ainsley!" he yelled at me, pain written across his face.

I pointed my finger at the girl as I advanced. "I said leave in the name of Jesus Christ, and leave this girl!"

The girl screwed her face up into a twisted visage before her eyes rolled into the back of her head, and she dropped onto the pavement. I ran back to Kyle, and as I knelt beside him for a moment, I thought I saw the figure of a man standing at the entryway into the alley. I looked away when Kyle groaned, and when I looked again, the man was gone. Kyle was holding his leg, and blood was soaking through the denim.

"What happened? What can I do?" Even as I asked, I was already pulling my cell phone out of my back pocket and calling 9-1-1.

Kyle leaned heavily on my arm, the pain getting to him. I was pretty sure he might pass out. "You did it, Reynolds," he mumbled. "You defeated Jai-ish."

~   ~   ~

Several hours later, the surgeon came out into the waiting room at the hospital to inform us that the surgery had gone well, although Kyle would be laid up for a while. Since his leg, his femur, no less, had been broken in two places with bone protruding through the skin, he would have to wear screws and plates until things healed. He would probably need surgery again. I swallowed hard when the surgeon mentioned that Kyle might have to use a cane for the rest of his life.

"But will he be okay? When can I see him?" I asked, Alec holding my hand.

"He will be fine, but after his recovery, he will need physical therapy. He will have some muscle weakness and pain for a while. I estimate that it will be at least six to twelve months before full recovery. Even then, as I said, he will probably need the assistance of a cane."

"A year," Mom whispered. She and Stephen had joined Alec and me at the hospital not long after we arrived. When the ambulance came for Kyle and the girl, who was still unconscious, officers at the station received the call. As soon as I mentioned Alec's name, one of the officers ran around to the building and told Alec.

"When can I see him?" I asked again.

"Does Mr. Drekr have any family here?"

Stephen shook his head. "The only relative still alive is his mother, and she lives in Los Angeles. We are the closest thing he has to a family. Ainsley is like his sister." He patted me on the shoulder.

"I see. Well, in that case, let him rest tonight, and you can visit him tomorrow," the surgeon said, directing his words at me.

I rode home with Mom and Stephen and then collapsed fully clothed into bed. I was asleep within minutes.

~ ~ ~

It was late morning before I awoke. It took a few seconds before I remembered the confrontation with Jai-ish, Kyle's broken leg, and the unconscious girl. As soon as I dressed, I decided to visit Kyle and the girl, whose name I still didn't know.

I checked the forecast on my phone and then chose a green and black plaid jumper dress with black leggings and black flats with silver hardware. I started to put my hair up into a bun but decided at the last minute to leave it down.

Stephen, Mom, and Ben were already in the kitchen, eating breakfast and talking about Kyle in the hospital. As far as Ben knew, Kyle fell in the alley last night and landed weird on his leg, breaking it. There was no need to mention how strong the femur bone actually is in the human body.

"Do you think they will let me in to see him?" Ben asked.

"I don't know, honey. I would think so since you're thirteen now." Mom handed Ben a plate of homemade waffles.

"Ainsley?" Mom asked, pointing at the fresh stack.

"No, thanks. I think I'm just going to grab a thermos of coffee and head over to the hospital. I want to see if they know who the girl is yet."

"What girl?" Ben asked.

"Um, they wheeled a girl about your age in last night. I think she was unconscious," I stammered.

Stephen picked up his coffee mug. "Go ahead to the hospital. Text us and let us know what you find out about her." Taking a sip of coffee, he added, "Maybe Ben knows her. Also, I need to talk to you later."

I knew what Stephen meant. For Malus Navis, he would need to record my story of the events that took place. Later, when Kyle was a little stronger, Stephen would record Kyle's story.

I heard a low meowing, and my eyes fell on Ben. He slowly looked up at me then towards the sliding glass doors that led to the wraparound deck. Angel's little shadow was visible through the sheer white curtains covering the glass. I snuck a peek at Mom and Stephen. Neither paid any attention.

Ben's eyes grew wide, but then he shrugged and dove back into his waffles.

I texted Alec once I was in my car. He said he would join me as soon as he took care of some things at the station. Once inside the hospital, I stopped by the gift shop and picked out a bouquet of charming wildly colored daisies and a succulent in a small white container that he could take back to L.A. I found a funny card that bordered on the inappropriate and almost got it because I knew Kyle would enjoy it. Then I remembered Eli Keach's words about purity and slid it back into the display.

When I walked in expecting to see a groaning-in-pain Kyle with his broken left leg, I found a smiling-like-a-fool Kyle talking to not *one*, not *two*, but *three* pretty nurses.

"Well, someone is feeling better," I said. All three nurses blushed, said hello, and then disappeared from the room.

"You scared them away with your flowers and candy."

"I didn't bring you candy. It's a cactus of some kind." I set the items on the tray nearest his bed.

"The gift shop sells candy too." Kyle winced as he leaned back onto his pillows.

"Ah, Grumpy Bunny, Kyle! It's so good to hear from you again."

Kyle growled with his eyes closed, then peeked out at me with one eye. "Sorry, we should be celebrating." He sat up a little straighter, winced, and leaned back again. "Grab my wallet and order us some real food. Whatever you want. The Wicked Jai-ish of the West is dead."

"Technically, not dead. Just delayed for a long while, hopefully."

"Whatever, Reynolds. Do you realize you are the only Seer ever to face him and live? Come up here." He patted the right side of the bed, close to his hip and away from the broken leg. He pulled my hand across his chest and over his rapidly beating heart, his light blue eyes searching my face. He hadn't shaved for a couple of days, and the stubble was beginning to grow a little darker than his celebrity highlighted blond hair.

"Reynolds, last night for a moment, I thought Jai-ish was going to kill me. I felt my leg break, and all he did was use the girl's body to blow me a kiss. But, you! You weren't affected by the demon. That says something about you."

"What?"

"You don't know how special you are."

Kyle studied my face and parted his lips slightly as if he was about to confess something to me. His hand still covered mine over his chest, and I was keenly aware that it felt heavy. Too close. I was leaning only inches from Kyle's upper half. A little flag went off in my head. Something with Kyle was changing, something I wasn't ready for at all.

Kyle swallowed, his voice dropping an octave. "Ainsley, I-"

"You only call me Ainsley when it's something bad."

"It's not bad. Not really. It's just that we have been together for-"

"Good, you're awake," Alec loudly announced as he walked in, thankfully, before Kyle could say something and make our friendly relationship awkward. I withdrew my hand and stood.

"Did you bring Kyle candy?" I asked as I moved away from the bed as casually as possible.

Alec looked confused. "Was I supposed to bring him candy?"

"No, he demanded it when I brought the flowers." I pointed to the bouquet.

Kyle picked up the vase of flowers and sniffed them, then met my stare over the bouquet. With a raised eyebrow, he said, "I never said *I* didn't like candy."

I stared at him. He was referencing an inside joke from a few years ago when he'd compared me to candy – pointing out that Alec didn't want anyone touching his candy. Why was he acting like this all of a sudden? Kyle and I had never liked *liked* each other. He knew Alec had a jealous streak – they'd come to blows once because of a misunderstanding – so why push him? What had come over him? Certainly, Kyle didn't have romantic feelings for me now?

"Is your morphine on a continuous I.V. drip?" I asked.

Kyle rolled his head around to look at the bag of liquid hanging near the bed. "Maybe…"

"Okay," Alec said slowly. "The reason I asked you both to come to the police station last night was that I found out that Mark Tahl, the Religious Studies professor, had been in Locklyn having meetings with Judge Rafe Kae."

"Rafe Kae? I met him the night that Tahl died."

"When?" Kyle and Alec asked in unison.

"As we were leaving the restaurant, Holland's. I ran into him in front of the restrooms." I fumbled in my handbag and then handed Rafe's business card to Alec. "I saw him again at the gym the other morning. Wonder what he was meeting with Tahl about?"

"I don't know, but it seems suspicious that he would run into you the night Tahl warned you about Jai-ish. Judge Kae was at the station last night at my request, but when I ran out to see what was happening in the alley, an officer told Kae to go home. After I leave here, I'm going to interview Kae and maybe run to the University of North Carolina at Chapel Hill to check out Tahl's office, talk to his peers, that sort of thing."

"I'll go with you," I said.

"Detective Wallace will go with me, Ainsley. She's my partner."

Kyle shifted in the bed, his leg in a cast to his hip, supported by cables hanging from the metal bar above him. "Jai-ish is gone. Reynolds expelled him. Why do you have to investigate anything?"

"Mark Tahl is still dead, Drekr. Someone pulled that trigger, and it's my job to find out who."

I looked up at Alec through my lashes. "What if you run across Professor Tahl's research on demons? Detective Wallace is going to ask questions when it falls outside of humanity's justice. Jai-ish isn't a threat anymore. Let me go with you – at least to Tahl's office."

Alec thought for a moment. "I'll make you a deal. Wallace and I interview Rafe Kae, and then you run with me to Tahl's office to search."

I reached for Alec's arm with a conniving smile growing across my face. He held up his index finger at me with an equally flirtatious grin. "But *I* speak with his staff. Not you."

I smiled. "Thank you, Alec."

I caught Kyle frowning at us, but then he threw on a smile and asked Alec about Detective Wallace. Maybe I read the situation with Kyle wrong. If he was asking about

Anita Wallace because he was still interested in her, then perhaps he was simply going to say something heartfelt to me, and I read too much into it. It wouldn't be the first time I'd jumped to a conclusion.

We visited with Kyle for a little longer until a nurse came to check things, then I made the excuse that I wanted to find the girl brought in last night. The nurse said she was in one of the rooms at the opposite end of the hall and to check at the nurse's station for the exact number.

Alec and I both slipped out and walked to the empty nurse's station.

"I guess we should wait until a nurse returns," I said, reading the names on the whiteboard and wondering which one was the girl.

Alec crossed his arms on the front counter and leaned back, resting his chin on his bicep so that he could speak to me quietly. "Ainsley, am I going to have to put Drekr down?"

"What? He's not a rabid dog." I let out a small laugh.

"I overheard him talking to you before I walked in. It wasn't going in a great direction. For me, anyway."

"Hey," I said as I placed my hand on Alec's cheek and rubbed my thumb reassuringly over the thick stubble. "We don't know what Kyle was going to say. He's on painkillers and probably strong sedatives too. No matter what he says, I love you. I'm in love with you, and I have been for the last four years."

"Is that right?" Alec nudged me with his shoulder.

"Yes. I'd kiss you, but-"

"Please, don't," a tired nurse with black hair standing on all ends stood on the other side of the desk. Alec and I both straightened. He showed her his badge as he cleared his throat.

"I'm Detective Graham with LPD. Last night, an ambulance brought in a young girl around twelve or thirteen with a possible head injury. Do you know anything about this?"

The woman studied his badge before making a big show of looking Alec up and down. Apparently, she approved because she sighed loudly and then motioned for us to follow her.

"Her name is Stacia. Stacia DeMeario. She's fourteen. She was brought in with a head wound. The paramedics found her unresponsive in an alleyway. We have tried reaching out to her folks to require them to come to the hospital, but the parents are drug addicts, from what I hear. The girl was dehydrated, malnourished, small for her age."

"How do you know her name then if no one has claimed her?"

"She's awake now. But it's a small town, Detective. One of the other nurses knows of her family. We notified the parents that she was here." The nurse stopped in front of a door and lowered her voice. "I think her parents believe she is better off here than at home."

"How sad," I said, my heart breaking for that little girl.

When the nurse walked away, Alec whispered to me, "She almost killed you. Are you sure you want to go inside?"

"She was possessed. To be fair, she almost killed Kyle."

Alec shrugged and opened the door. "No reason to hold a grudge over that."

~ ~ ~

The girl in the bed appeared smaller than she had in the dark alley last night. Perhaps it was because she was no longer wearing her off-white puffer jacket and big toboggan. Instead, Stacia wore a hospital gown with blanket upon blanket on the bed.

"Stacia?" Alec's voice was gentle and low.

The girl on the bed with the raven black hair, watching the small television attached to the wall, rolled her eyes over at us. Her eyes were different than last night. Even in the dark alley, I could make out the reflective nature of the demon's eyes, but here at the hospital now, her eyes were brown – a sad, lonely brown.

"Stacia, I'm Detective Alec Graham with the Locklyn Police Department. My friends, Ainsley and Kyle, found you last night and called the paramedics." Alec placed his hand on my lower back and pushed me forward a bit so Stacia could see me. "Do you remember seeing Ainsley last night?"

She cleared her throat as she struggled to sit up in bed, a bandage covering her right temple from where she'd fallen on the cold and unforgiving pavement.

"I'm sorry, I don't remember much from yesterday. Or even the last couple of days. I remember walking home from the library. I'd gone there to do my homework because we don't have the internet at my house. Oh, have they found my backpack yet? My school tablet is in it."

"I'm afraid not yet," Alec answered. "You didn't have anything with you last night."

"I need to find it. My parents can't afford to have it replaced."

I stepped forward. "I'm a student-teacher. There is usually insurance covering a lost or damaged tablet. For a small deposit."

The girl looked down at her hands crossed over her lap. "My parents couldn't afford the insurance."

Alec sat down at the foot of Stacia's bed. "Stacia, don't worry about your tablet. I'll make sure that we either find it or get you a new one from the school. You won't have to pay anything. I promise I'll take care of that for you. Can you tell me what you do remember? Did you talk to anyone at the library or on your way home?"

Stacia's brow furrowed, then she reached up and cautiously touched her bandage. "It's weird. It's like a part of my memory is gone. When I try to think too hard on it, my head starts to throb."

"That's okay." Alec handed her the card with his contact info on it. "If you do remember anything, even something small, will you call me?"

The girl nodded as Alec stood, but then the door opened, and a woman in her mid-forties briskly walked in. "Hi, I'm Ellen Sears, the social worker here at the hospital. The nurse said that you were in here questioning Stacia, a *minor*, without her parents present." She emphasized the word minor, and I at once disliked her.

Alec held his hand out to the woman. "I'm Detective Graham with the LPD, but the nurse misunderstood our reason for being here. This is Ainsley Reynolds. She and the gentleman down the hall, Kyle Drekr, found Stacia in the alley around the corner from the police station last night. Since we were already on this floor, we wanted to stop in and check on her."

The woman studied Alec's face, gave me a once-over, and then apparently approved of our reason. "Well, since Stacia's parents are no-shows, we will need to arrange for state care when she is released."

"No, please," Stacia said, holding her hand to her temple again. "I don't want to go back to foster care. Seriously, if you just let me go home, I'll be fine. I'm old enough to take care of myself."

Ellen Sears gave the girl a bittersweet smile. "You're fourteen, Stacia. You're too young to stay on your own, especially after head trauma."

Alec cleared his throat. "Miss Sears, may I speak with you out in the hall, please?"

Miss Sears recovered quickly from her look of shock. "Of course, Detective."

Alec motioned for me to stay with Stacia while he and the tall woman left the room, shutting the door behind them. I sat down at the foot of Stacia's bed, where Alec had just been moments ago.

"Stacia, I know you don't know me, but I've seen you walking around town before. I found you last night in the alley. What I am saying is that you can trust me. Is everything all right at home?"

Stacia's brown eyes blinked, tears staying firmly in place, refusing to trickle down her cheeks. "It could be better. But home is better than foster care. You can trust me on that."

"Maybe Detective Graham can work something out for you. He knows a lot of people, good people."

Stacia shrugged, and I had a feeling this swapping between homes had been a way of life for her.

Alec returned without the severe-looking Ms. Sears. He shut the hospital room door firmly before coming to stand beside Stacia's bed.

"Okay, Stacia, I spoke with Ms. Sears, and she has agreed after your release from the hospital to make arrangements for you to stay with my family until things get sorted, if that's all right with you, of course?"

"Your family?" Stacia said, looking Alec up and down, wide-eyed.

"Well, not me. My grandfather passed away last year, and his friend Tilda is the woman who raised my father. She also raised me. Now she lives alone in a huge house, and she would welcome you with open arms. She didn't have any children of her own and always wanted a girl in the house."

"Really? Where is your house? I mean, her house?"

"It's in South Carolina, but Ms. Sears said crossing the state line won't be an issue for you since it is an emergency, and I promised to bring you back for hearings, meetings, and such. Of course, she will go to the house and check it out as well as interview Tilda before you are released, but I don't see this as being a problem."

"Would that work, Stacia?" I asked with a hopeful smile on my face.

The girl nodded. "I think so. Does she have internet? Would I go to school there? Does she have a spare bedroom?"

Alec smiled, probably the widest I'd ever seen. "Yes, Tilda has internet. Since this is considered a temporary move, Ms. Sears said you could stay enrolled in the county and do virtual work from the house in South Carolina. As for a spare bedroom, you will have your pick of any of nine bedrooms. And if you want it redecorated, Tilda will see to it."

"Wow! Really?"

"Yes," Alec leaned down and patted her head. "But right now, Ainsley and I have to leave. I've got some work to get done today. If you remember anything else, call me. Ainsley, why don't you write down your number for Stacia too? That way, she can reach you."

I jotted my cell phone number down on the notepad beside the phone. Stacia smiled at me with a huge smile before we left.

"Thank you so much!"

As I smiled back at her and turned to go out the door, I finally saw that tear run down her cheek.

# CHAPTER TEN

"**E**ver heard of the phrase *in like Flynn?*" I asked Alec as we walked to the SUV.

"I have," he answered, opening the passenger side door for me. "Not sure I understand you referencing the actor Errol Flynn however."

"I studied film in college as an elective." Instead of climbing in, I leaned against his chest and kissed him, not a quick kiss either, a long and passionate kiss right there in the parking garage.

Alec studied my face when I pulled away. "What was that for?" he asked in a husky voice.

"For what you are doing for Stacia. Does Tilda even know she is going to have a teenage girl living with her?"

"I texted her before I walked back into Stacia's room. She's more than fine with it. Tilda has a heart of gold."

I climbed into the truck and pulled on my seatbelt. Alec got in and started the engine. I was thankful for the blast of heat as this December afternoon was turning colder by the hour.

"Plus, Tilda knows I would never send a problem to her. Ms. Sears said Stacia has been bounced around to several homes since she was four. Her parents clean up for a while and then go right back to drugs eventually. Despite that, the girl maintains a 4.0 GPA by going to the library for homework and using every available school resource. You saw her. She's scared to death that she's lost her school's iPad."

I smiled. "She has no idea that a millionaire's family is going to be the ones fostering her. I hope she has a good Christmas." I ran my hand over Alec's as he maneuvered the truck out of its parking spot.

"Multimillionaire," he said, adjusting the gear shift from reverse to drive.

"What?" My voice barely over a whisper. Surely, I'd misheard him.

"When my grandfather passed away, if you include his assets and real estate, my trust fund, all of the investments, plus other income, then it's a multimillionaire's family, as in triple-digit-millionaire.

According to Fred, Grandfather's personal investor, projections show billionaire in five years."

My mouth hung open. I could not even conceive such a thing. "Yet, you still want to do this? Solve murders? Have a Police Chief yell at you?"

Alec glanced over at me as he drove. "Just for as long as I am physically able, Ainsley. One day, I won't be able to, then I will sit back and do whatever rich people do, I guess. Although my grandfather never stopped working after retiring as a surgeon, he never stopped creating businesses and jobs. I think he was still working up until the week he passed away. And who knows? Maybe we can use the estate to house foster kids."

I considered his words for a few minutes before asking the question that had been plaguing me for four years. "Alec, did you pay my outstanding balance at the college my Freshman year?"

He frowned, his jaw clenching.

I pushed on. "Did you cover my expenses, what the GI bill didn't cover, the last four years? You're the only other person that could have afforded such a huge expense. Kyle denies it was him."

Alec tapped his thumb on the steering wheel.

"Alec?"

He sighed loudly. "I'm not sure what I should say. If I tell you no, then you find out differently, you're going to be mad that I lied to you. If I say yes, then you're going to be mad that I interfered in your life."

"Pull the truck over."

'Ainsley-"

"I said pull the truck over."

"We're almost to your street."

"Now, Alec. Please."

Alec sighed and pulled the SUV over. He put the gear in park and turned to look at me as if bracing for impact. Instead, I placed my hand on the back of his neck and pulled his face close to mine.

"Thank you," I whispered. "Thank you for doing that for me. If you hadn't, then I would have had to wait at least another year before going to school to give me time to work and earn the funds. Then I would have had to work every evening, every summer, and every Christmas break. Instead, I was able to study. I'm on the Dean's List."

"I know," he whispered back.

"You're right. I would have been angry four years ago if I'd known. I'm a different person now. I see the bigger picture now."

Alec smiled, searching my eyes. "Good, because everything I own belongs to you except for the estate in South Carolina. I willed that to Tilda."

I sat back in alarm. "You did what?"

"My line of work is dangerous, Ainsley. I willed everything to you in the event of my death. The estate will go to Tilda unless she is no longer here, then you will receive it in addition to everything else."

"Alec. I don't know what to say." My mind was whirling too fast to focus on one thought, let alone form a real coherent sentence.

"I love you, Ainsley. I have for a long time now. I want to marry you, but I haven't found the right time to ask you yet."

My eyes grew even wider. "You could ask me now."

Alec laughed. "In my truck, on the side of the road, less than a block from your mother's house?"

"Yes."

"I don't have the ring with me."

"There's a ring?" I could barely hear my voice.

"Of course, there's a ring. Do you think my Southern upbringing is going to let me ask you to marry me without a ring?" He sounded incredulous as he turned toward the steering wheel again to continue our drive to Mom's house.

"I don't care about a ring. My answer is yes. I mean, when you ask me, I'm going to say yes."

Alec's smile grew. "Good to know. But I still have to officially ask you."

"You could have asked me at the cabin this past weekend."

"I almost did. Then I got to thinking that you might get so excited that you would have kissed me, and then one thing might have led to another." He threw me a sideways glance. "I thought we would wait until our wedding night. You know, because we both committed to Christ, and it seems…I don't know… appropriate now."

I slowly nodded my head. He was right. "Okay, but then you need to ask me soon. We should plan for a small ceremony in the spring."

He laughed. "In the spring? Would that be enough time to plan everything? I haven't even asked you yet." He parked the truck in front of Mom's house.

"Look, if we are waiting until our wedding night after we have already been waiting *four years*, then let's not waste time planning a wedding. I'm happy with a small ceremony and a beautiful, dazzling Vera Wang gown."

Alec kissed me quickly on the lips before opening his door. "Well, then, I'd better get to work on finding the perfect time to ask you."

~ ~ ~

I had to wait an hour and a half for Alec and Detective Wallace to meet with Judge Rafe Kae and talk with each other about the case. Alec sent Wallace on a mission to do something else while we were at the University of North Carolina at Chapel Hill to search Tahl's office.

Finally, Alec pulled up in front of the house around 3pm dressed in dress pants, a tailored shirt, a suit jacket, and a black coat. He glanced at my outfit as he held the SUV door open for me.

"You changed clothes. Is that what you are wearing to the school? Won't you get cold?"

"Cold in this?" Waving my hand innocently over my black knit sheath sweater dress, a black peacoat, and black ankle boots. I'd somehow forgotten to wear leggings again. "We will be in your heated truck and then inside a heated building."

"You amaze me," Alec said, stealing a kiss from me as I climbed into the truck. "After all these years, you are still driving me crazy."

"Hopefully, you will feel the same way in fifty years." I made a face at Alec, and he laughed.

"The good Lord only knows how I'll stand it," he said as he shut the door.

After we merged onto the highway, I asked Alec about his meeting with Rafe. "He said that he has a personal interest in Religious Studies and demons specifically. I recorded the meeting. Normally, I wouldn't share it with an unauthorized individual, but considering that you are involved anyway, you might want to hear it."

I felt the excitement leap up into my chest. "Of course, I want to hear it."

Alec pulled his phone from his jacket pocket. "Here. It's under audio dated today. Go to the beginning."

I found his recording app and scrolled in reverse until I reached the start of the recording.

Alec's voice: *This is Detective Alec Graham and Detective Anita Wallace with the Honorable Judge Rafe Kae in his office. Judge Kae, thank you for seeing us. I want to ask you about a man by the name of Mark Tahl. Do you recognize that name?*

Rafe: *(clearing his throat) Yes, Dr. Tahl is a Professor of Religious Studies at Chapel Hill. I have a personal interest in religion, demons, and angels – those topics within the supernatural realm – so I have reached out to the professor with questions in the past. However, this particular meeting he requested due to some research he conducted that he thought might be of interest to me.*

Alec: *That being?*

Rafe: *Detective Graham, I understand that you are investigating Dr. Tahl's murder, but I think you will find this information a bit ridiculous in your line of work.*

Alec: *You would be surprised. In our line of work, we have heard it all.*

Rafe: *(taking a deep breath) Yes, I am sure you have. Dr. Tahl learned of an ancient demon who, legend has it, led armies as an angel. He was a much-loved general of the armies of Heaven, but, alas, he wanted more. This angel chose to fall. Tahl believed that this fallen angel, now a demon, could cross between this plane and the others.*

Detective Wallace: *What do you mean by this plane and the others?*

Rafe: *This plane is the reality that we know. We can see it, hear it. We follow its rules of time and space. Other planes separate this plane from Heaven. Or, Hell in some cases.*

Alec: *Another realm. A spiritual realm.*

Rafe: *I see you have heard it all.*

Alec: *Please continue.*

Rafe: *This demon can move back and forth between planes – realms – and possess people. The reason Tahl came to me was that he was under the impression that this demon had sent a message about a young woman in our town.*

I glanced at Alec, his eyes still glued to the road.

Wallace: *Had someone approached Dr. Tahl with this message? Was it a legitimate threat?*

Rafe: *Hmm. I realize Dr. Tahl was shot. But do you plan to order an autopsy? Have you received the report yet? Have you seen his body?*

Alec: *We were the investigators at the crime scene. We have ordered an autopsy per procedure, but no results yet. We already know the cause of death. Why?*

Rafe: *The reason I ask is that Dr. Tahl woke up with cuts across his upper thigh a few days before his death. He asked me to look at it. The cuts formed a sentence in Arabic.*

Wallace: *Arabic?*

Alec: *Tell us more about this message.*

Rafe: *Dr. Tahl and I both specialize in ancient Arabic. As I told you, it is a hobby of mine. I looked at the cuts on his leg, and my translation was the same as hi*s.

Wallace: *What was your translation?*

Rafe: *(quiet for a long moment, then another deep breath) It read, 'Jai-ish names Ainsley Grace Reynolds.'*

I heard an intake of breath that I was sure had been Alec's. I, on the other hand, had stopped breathing altogether. I paused the recording as I forced my lungs to inhale.

"So, Jai-ish carved my name into Mark Tahl's leg? Do we know that for sure?"

Alec pulled my hand into his. "I sent Detective Wallace to the coroner. Even if he hasn't had a chance to finish the autopsy, he can at least confirm what Judge Kae said is true about the cuts and provide her with photographic evidence. Ainsley, if Dr. Tahl was mentally disturbed, he could have done that to himself. Judge Kae said they both knew the written language."

"What does Detective Wallace think?"

"At first, she was leaning toward the mental disorder theory, but then her paranormal curiosity kicked in, and she started throwing out other theories. It doesn't help that the young woman named just happens to be my girlfriend."

He'd referred to me as his girlfriend. I played the recording again.

Wallace: *Did you say, Ainsley Reynolds? Isn't that-*

Alec: *Yes. Judge Kae, could Dr. Tahl have done that to himself?*

Rafe: *I suppose if he were the type of man to do so. However, Dr. Tahl was a man of integrity with no signs of mental illness. He was not a man to play games.*

Alec: *Are you a man who plays games?* (a long drawn-out silence) *This young woman, Ainsley Reynolds, mentioned that she met you at Holland's Steakhouse less than thirty minutes before Dr. Tahl approached her on the street.*

Rafe: *I did meet Miss Reynolds at the restaurant shortly before Dr. Tahl's demise. I was quite shocked when she introduced herself. I gave her my card in hopes that she would reach out to me.*

(A rustling sound.)

Alec: *This card?*

Rafe: *Yes. I am beginning to understand that you and Miss Reynolds are very close.*

Alec: *I'm just trying to figure out why her name was cut into a man's leg, and then that same man would go out of his way to give her a message before someone killed him.*

Rafe: *I can help you with that. That is if you are to believe in the stories that Dr. Tahl researched.*

Wallace: *Please tell us.*

Alec: *Before you explain to us Dr. Tahl's theories, did he happen to work with other people on these theories? Do you know of anyone who would want to harm the professor?*

Rafe: *Dr. Tahl has – had – two teaching assistants who also worked as researchers. He depended on both of them a great deal, but I would hardly suspect that either one would want any harm to befall the professor.*

"Stop the audio for a second," Alec said. I paused the recording as I waited for him to explain.

"Does it seem odd to you the way Judge Kae speaks?"

I shrugged. "He sounds dignified. The way I would assume a judge would speak."

"Hmm. I've dealt with judges both for business and when I was younger, not to mention my grandfather was friends with a few. There is nothing informal about Rafe Kae. He's only a few years older than me, but he sounds much older."

"Perhaps he was mentored by someone older and picked it up from him or her. What do we know about him?"

Alec tapped his thumb on the steering wheel again. "The background search showed the usual, what you would expect from an attorney turned judge. He grew up in Boston, attended Harvard, did extremely well. Wealthy family. He won every case that ever went to trial as an attorney, which in itself is rare. He's one of the youngest judges. He has a reputation for being fair, according to the people we interviewed at the courthouse. Everyone seems to like him," he glanced at me before continuing, "especially the women."

"Well, of course. He's swoon-worthy." I shoved Alec's arm when he frowned at me. Then I leaned over and kissed his cheek. "But he is no Alec Graham."

Alec shook his head as he looked out the windshield, but I saw the smallest of smiles play on his lips. Once I knew Alec was satisfied with my answer, I went back to the recording.

Detective Wallace: *Can you give us the names of the assistants?*

Rafe: *If I remember correctly, Thomas and Nadine. I do not believe Dr. Tahl ever provided me with their last names.*

Wallace: *Thomas and Nadine?*

Rafe: *Yes. I know the professor had them researching as much as they could find out about this demon. His name is Jai-ish, although he has gone by many names in the past. According to legend and Dr. Tahl's theories, unlike other demons who run errands and follow orders, Jai-ish can move quickly between the realms at will. Whereas other demons can merely influence people's actions, Jai-ish can fully possess them for the time being. He can also leave them unharmed and alive, although if the person possessed does not repent of any sin, then Jai-ish can return to the body in the future.*

Wallace: *Dr. Tahl believed this legend?*

Rafe: *Yes, completely. If he doubted, all doubts were erased when he awoke with the inscription in his flesh.*

Wallace: *What does this have to do with Ainsley Reynolds?*

Alec held up his hand, and I paused the recording. "What you can't see is that Judge Kae looked directly at me before he answered. I think he knows more about my relationship with you than he let on in the beginning."

I ran my hand over his before I touched the play button again.

Rafe: (taking a deep breath) *Again, according to legend, God gifted men with spiritual gifts and talents. Some men were given the spiritual gift of discernment – and by men, I mean mankind – to see and hear beings, not of this realm. This includes the spirits of those trapped on Earth for whatever reason, demons, Nephilim, and other…things. Every once in a while, a person bestowed with this gift can concentrate on it fully and become powerful. So powerful, in fact, that the demons in the other realm can see them shining in this realm.*

Alec: (in a whispered voice) *A beacon.*

Rafe: *Yes. THE Beacon. This person can command demons back to Hell with only mere words.*

Wallace: *What does this have to do with Ainsley Reynolds?*

Rafe: *Dr. Tahl believed that Miss Reynolds is the Beacon who Jai-ish has seen. If this is true, then she is in great danger. Every Beacon who Jai-ish has battled has died a horrible death.* (The sound of a chair creaking) *If you wish, I could go with you to the University to speak with Thomas and Nadine. Dr. Tahl learned more about this story.*

Alec: *That is all right, Your Honor. I'm sure you have better things to do.*

Rafe: *Better things than saving a woman's life? I should pray not. Miss Reynolds is different from all the other Beacons. She is not alone.*

Alec: *What do you mean?*

Rafe: *If she is the Beacon, she is the first Beacon with the spiritual gift passed down to her through lineage. This multiplies her power, making her a stronger opponent for Jai-ish. He will consider her a challenge that he cannot allow to escape him.*

Alec: *How would you know if she was this Beacon and if it was part of her lineage?*

Rafe: *Allow me to accompany you to the University, and I can show you. I assure you, Detective Graham, we want the same thing – for Miss Reynolds to remain safe and defeat Jai-ish. If you believe the story is true, of course.*

The recording stopped.

"That's it? What happened?"

Alec shrugged. "I shut off the recording at that point because the interview was over. However, I did relent. Judge Kae will meet us at the school this evening." He squeezed my hand. "I want to know what he thinks he knows about your family, your father. I want to know who *he* is in all of this. I don't think this is just an interest to him, a hobby. Fishing is a hobby. Gaming is a hobby. Cosplay is a hobby. Demonology is *not* a hobby."

I thought about Ben. Kyle and I had kept Ben's dead cat sighting to ourselves, but what if Rafe and Dr. Tahl were correct? What if the reason Jai-ish was able to see me so easily was that I had inherited my father's power as well as my own?

"But I defeated Jai-ish. You're only searching for Dr. Tahl's murderer now, right?"

"I am," Alec said, pulling me closer to him and wrapping his arm around my shoulders as he drove. "But what if the next demon who sees you is stronger and more dangerous than Jai-ish?"

# CHAPTER ELEVEN

ark Tahl's office was a historian's dream come true and a born-organized person's worst nightmare. I couldn't find any organization among his stacks of papers, books, scrolls, photographs, or maps scattered about the room on bookshelves, desks, and even on the floor. Documents and pictures covered every square inch of the paneled walls. I had no idea how the man ever graded papers in the mess.

Alec had gone into another room to interview Dr. Tahl's assistants, Thomas and Nadine. Although he had expected to meet Rafe here, the handsome judge was nowhere to be found.

I slumped down into the professor's chair and looked at the stacks of papers, many of which were students' papers needing graded. How was I supposed to find out what Mark Tahl knew if I couldn't find anything in this room? *God, if a more dangerous adversary is coming, please help me find what I need in this room. Help me to prepare.*

"Miss Reynolds?"

I jumped at the sound of Rafe's voice. "Rafe! You startled me."

The judge walked into the room wearing a tailored three-piece wool suit. I had never seen a man his age wear one as pristine as his, though. It was as if servants had dressed him this evening; not one thing was out of place. He carried a black trench coat slung neatly over his arm.

"Seems odd being in the professor's office without him here," Rafe observed as he slowly draped his coat over the back of a chair filled with papers.

"I've been here for about thirty minutes, and I can't make sense of anything. There's no organization."

Rafe ran his hand lightly over a sheaf of papers. "Where are his assistants?"

"Talking to Alec."

Rafe turned, curiosity crossing his face. "Alec? Oh, yes, Detective Graham." He smiled at me as if he knew something. The hairs on the back of my neck rose. I stood in response, my body preparing to either take flight through the office door at the end of the room or to fight whatever threat my mind conjured. I needed to get a grip.

"Do you know where Dr. Tahl would have kept his research on Jai-ish?" I asked, trying to calm my rapidly beating heart and keep my voice steady.

"I believe so. Am I making you feel uncomfortable? Miss Reynolds, you have nothing to fear from me." He cocked his head, waiting for my answer.

"No, of course not. It's just been a long week. Anxiety and all." I plastered a smile on my face as I looked down at the papers on the desk.

"Would you prefer for me to wait out in the hall until Detective Graham finishes speaking with Thomas and Nadine?"

I don't know why his question caught me off guard, most likely because he was so considerate of my feelings.

I laughed a bit uneasily. "No, Rafe. I'm fine. It's not you. It's definitely me."

Rafe frowned slightly and nodded his head. However, the small smile on his face told me that he didn't believe me. "No, I shall wait in the hall until your friend returns. I believe I am overwhelming your senses."

"Please, don't go," I said, taking a tentative step toward him, but even as I did, my spine stiffened in response.

Rafe raised his eyes to look at me, studying my face. "Has Detective Graham told you about our conversation this afternoon?"

"About me being a Beacon? I've heard that before."

"You have fought the demons before as a Beacon of Light."

It wasn't a question. Judge Rafe Kae did not appear shocked, or doubtful, or cynical. He was completely calm as if observing a gorilla through the plexiglass window at the zoo, assuredly safe from the danger.

"I have. I know about the spiritual gift of discernment. We call them Seers."

He didn't move, didn't nod. His sapphire blue eyes studied me.

"Alec told me that Mark Tahl received a message about Jai-ish carved into his leg. It was a message with my name attached. But, there is nothing to worry about. I expelled Jai-ish last night."

"Do you truly believe that a human can expel a demon of Jai-ish's caliber quickly in a dark alley?"

"How do you know it was in the alley?"

"I was with Detective Graham when an officer came into the room. I overheard the man tell the detective that something had happened in the alley and that you were involved. Detective Graham did not hesitate but ran out of the room. Now, you say, you expelled Jai-ish. I do not believe that is the case."

I took a step backward away from Rafe as I considered his words. "He used a girl's body to hurt my friend, my Protector and tried to hurt me. It didn't work. I watched the demon leave her body."

"What did he look like when he left her body?"

"I mean, I didn't see a form or anything. The alley was dark. The girl shrieked and then dropped to the ground. I talked to her this morning. She's not possessed."

Rafe turned toward the bookcase again and pulled open a drawer. He began rifling through the papers inside until he found a yellow sheet inside a plastic cover sleeve. He handed it to me. The writing was indecipherable.

"It is in Arabic. The translation reads that Jai-ish commanded armies. He gave orders to thousands of demons."

I looked up from the paper to Rafe, who had taken a step toward me. I made myself stand perfectly still, although my mind was screaming at me to move away.

"This states that Jai-ish can order another demon of a higher power into the body of a human. I do not think that you expelled Jai-ish last night. I believe that Jai-ish wanted to see what abilities you possess, and he observed you banishing another demon."

I swallowed.

"You are the first Beacon – Seer, as you call yourself – to come from the same lineage. Was your father not one?"

"He was," I whispered.

"And your brother?"

I jerked my head up quickly. "How do you know about Ben?" I demanded with as much force in my voice as I could manage.

However, Rafe was undisturbed by my anger. Once again, he viewed me as the new animal at the zoo. "If your father possessed the gift, as you do, it is only natural for your brother to possess the ability. You both share the same father, do you not? How old is he?"

I deeply inhaled before I answered. "Thirteen."

A smile played on Rafe's face. "Ah, yes. The Jews believe that is the age of right and wrong. He will begin to come into his ability. He will need guidance."

"How do you know this?"

Rafe touched the paper in my hand with the tip of his index finger. "It is all there. Do not be complacent. Jai-ish still sees you. He is observing your strengths and weaknesses. He means to kill you."

The humming in my head took on a static sound, and instinctively I retreated behind the desk again, placing space between myself and Rafe.

"Are you him? Are you Jai-ish?" My voice sounded strong, but I slid the paper onto the desk before concealing my trembling hands in the pockets of my dress.

Rafe turned fully to face me, shoving his own hands into the pockets of his trousers. My guess so that I wouldn't feel threatened by him. "I am not Jai-ish. I am not here to harm you, Miss Reynolds. I want to help you defeat him."

"It's just that when I'm around you, I feel-"

"Everything all right?" Alec asked from the door of the office with Thomas and Nadine behind him.

I nodded. "Of course. Rafe was just explaining this paper to me."

Warily, Alec regarded the judge as he walked around him. He took the paper from me.

"What language is this?"

"Arabic," Rafe answered. He continued to explain to Alec everything he had shared with me about his theory that Jai-ish commanded another demon into Stacia to observe my reactions and strategy. He also told Alec that he believed that Ben was also a Beacon, a Seer.

Thomas, a young man about my age with a scruffy blond beard and wearing a brown beanie, went to the bookshelves and removed another sheet of paper. I stood stunned as Nadine, a redheaded woman a little younger than Thomas, said, "Not that one," and pulled out another sheet of yellowed paper encased in plastic. How could they find anything in this chaos?

"This is the document that Dr. Tahl was translating last," Nadine said as she handed the paper to Rafe.

"How long will it take you to translate it?" Alec asked.

"I'm reading it now," Rafe answered calmly. Alec and I exchanged glances, and I figured he was thinking the same thing I was. Neither of us was an expert in ancient languages, but shouldn't Rafe be looking in books or writing something down? Doesn't translating ancient text take time and study?

Rafe cleared his throat. "Jai-ish has battled many Beacons in the past, Seers as you call them. All of the gifted men have died during the confrontation. The only time banishment succeeded with Jai-ish was after a battle with an archangel. The battle lasted three days, and the two human men involved, a Seer and Protector, both died on the first day, although they did weaken Jai-ish to some degree. According to this detailed script, the writer makes the assumption that if a Seer is to expel Jai-ish to Hell for any length of time, the Seer would require other Seers and Protectors, and an archangel."

"Is that all?" Alec asked dryly.

Rafe half-smiled at him. "I have told you everything I know. What can you share with me about the organization Malus Navis and its current Seers?"

My eyes skimmed over Thomas and Nadine. I didn't know either of them. "I don't know what you're talking about, Rafe."

"Thomas? Nadine? If the detective is finished with his questions, would you please leave us?"

Thomas and Nadine both looked at Alec, waiting for his permission.

After a moment's hesitation, Alec nodded his head. "I have your contact information. Thank you."

The young man and woman exchanged glances, hesitating only a moment before nodding to Rafe as they silently left the room.

"That was odd," I whispered to Alec.

Alec sat down on the edge of the desk. "Why should we tell you anything about Malus Navis?"

"I have studied demons and angels for years. I am perhaps the only one that can help you, Detective Graham."

Rafe turned to me. "We are alone now, Miss Reynolds, except for your friend." He lifted a stack of papers from the chair near the desk and moved them to the floor. After wiping the seat with his hand, he sat down.

With a quick glance at Alec, my eyes landed on Rafe. I began, "What do you know about Malus Navis and my father?"

"It is an organization consisting of religious leaders, men with the gift of discernment, and men with the gift to travel between realms. God called you to the gift at the age of thirteen. However, your father did not recognize it in you until you were fifteen. Unfortunately, Gerald Reynolds died from complications following a vehicle accident without telling you anything about your ability, the organization, or even about Jesus the Christ."

Rafe continued, "Fortunately for you, your inner circle grew to include people strong in their faith and pivotal in your journey – Maren Bell, Stephen Reeves, and Kyle Drekr. All members of the organization."

"How could you possibly know all of that?" Alec said, leaning toward Rafe.

"Detective, like you, I use my resources wisely. I am a judge, remember?"

"Okay," I said slowly. "There doesn't seem to be much you don't know about Malus Navis."

"If you need to call upon more Seers, how many can you depend on to come to your aid?"

"I don't know. I have never met another one. Kyle is a Protector and the closest one to a Seer that I know."

"Are you aware that you are the first female Seer in history?" Rafe asked, cocking his head at me again.

"No, I didn't know that. No one has ever said anything."

"It cannot be a coincidence, Miss Reynolds. You inherited the gift from your father, perhaps for such a time as this. It will take you combining your ability with another Seer to defeat Jai-ish in this realm."

"But that won't kill him. He will just come back and possess another person," Alec said, turning to look out the office window.

"True. However, the document states it took Jai-ish hundreds of years to regain his strength after the last banishment. There is an excellent chance that the Christ will return before Jai-ish can walk in this realm again."

"Rafe, I don't have an archangel in my pocket." I raised my eyebrows at him and tugged at the empty pockets of my dress.

"Hm. We will look into that for you. In the meantime, you should meet with the elders and learn who you can depend on to help you."

Alec turned to face Rafe. "What do you mean *we* will look into that for you?"

"I have resources, Detective."

"I'd like the name of your resources."

"Not possible, I am afraid. Just as you have informants, I do as well."

Alec's jaw clenched. "You have informants who know about archangels and demons?" The sarcasm was almost tangible.

"Yes. You must trust me, Detective, if Jai-ish is to be defeated. The longer he roams the Earth, the more strength he gains."

"And you get this info from these documents? For the record, I don't trust you, Judge Kae. I would advise you not to leave Locklyn after you return."

"If that is your wish."

Alec rolled his shoulders back. "We don't know when Jai-ish will strike *if* this is all true. Will he possess the girl Stacia again, or choose a different victim?"

Rafe frowned. "Not victim. Vessel. He did not possess the girl before as that was another demon, I believe. He will choose someone else. Perhaps someone close to you who you would not suspect. I am trying to solve how a demon was able to possess the girl. You said she is fourteen?"

I nodded.

"She knows right from wrong, but for a demon to possess her means that she had to have given in to something, some sin that she could not turn from."

Alec answered him. "Stacia comes from a hard home life. We don't know the particulars, other than she has been in several foster homes over the past decade. Her parents are drug addicts."

"Ah, I see now. If the girl Stacia took a particular drug or someone snuck something to her that caused her to lose herself, then the demon may have slipped in. It is not her sin then, but her mind that opened itself. I am certain it was against her will."

"Where are you getting this? From the document?" I asked. "I think you need to talk with Stephen. It seems you know more than the leaders of Malus Navis."

Rafe gave me that half-smile again. "I told you. I have a personal interest in Religious Studies. I have been studying every document and parchment for as long as I can remember."

~ ~ ~

Alec and I left the school after we were sure Rafe had driven away in his Bentley. Neither one of us spoke at first as Alec drove. The heat was on high, and I pulled a fleece blanket from the backseat onto my bare legs and crossed them. I silently chastised myself for wearing the dress again with no leggings to get Alec's attention. He certainly wouldn't want to marry a frozen popsicle.

"Are you cold?" Alec asked.

"A little. I think it is more from what Rafe told us than the temperature in the truck."

"I think there is more to Judge Kae than we know, but I'm not sure how to go about finding out. I'm still no closer to finding Mark Tahl's shooter."

"You didn't get anywhere with Thomas and Nadine?"

"No, not really. They both seemed to respect and admire the professor. Neither owns a gun and now they are uncertain about their future as TAs since Tahl was the only one teaching Religious Studies."

"Does Rafe own a gun?"

"No. The only person involved in this case with a registered gun is you. I'm choosing to look past that because I know you didn't shoot him."

"Gee, thanks, Detective."

"The bullet was from a .308. Unless you have an unregistered military-grade weapon under your dress, I don't believe it was you. The shot came from 100 yards away. Someone was trailing Mark Tahl and used the opportunity to silence him."

I frowned. "A .308? One of those rifles you can set up on a tripod?"

"Yes. A pawn shop near the University reported a break in about a week before the shooting. One of the items missing from the back room: a .308."

I bit my lip as I looked out the window. I knew one person with a .308. I had just seen him with it last week while I was in West Virginia expelling a demon and turning in the sex traffickers. Alec didn't have any reason to run a background check on Stephen. What was I thinking? Stephen was still in Charleston when someone shot Tahl. It couldn't have been him. I shivered.

Alec rubbed the blanket over my knee as if the gesture would warm me. "Does this help?" he whispered.

He needed to propose soon, for crying out loud. "Not unless you want to pull the SUV over."

Alec removed his hand as he laughed. "I'm not going to propose to you in my truck."

"We are always in your truck, Alec," I answered with the slightest tone of aggravation.

"Do you want me to pick you up in the morning?"

"What are you thinking?" I knew he could hear the hope in my voice.

"I figured you would want to tell Kyle tomorrow about what we learned before I have to report to the station. I'll check in with Wallace tonight to see if she can confirm the cuts on Mark Tahl's leg."

"You should go straight to the station in the morning. I'll drive over to the hospital and talk to Kyle."

"Are you sure?"

"Yeah. Maybe he knows about more Seers within the organization."

"Stephen will know."

"I'll fill him in tonight unless he is already asleep."

~ ~ ~

It was late by the time Alec dropped me off in front of the house. When he opened the passenger door of the SUV, he started to walk me up, but I told him no. Everyone was asleep from the look of the house, and I didn't want to wake anyone. Instead, I gave him a quick kiss and started up the steps, but Alec pulled me back and kissed me passionately.

He moved his lips to my ear. "I promise you. Soon."

I squeezed his hand as he turned to leave. I silently prayed that God would grant my request to live long enough to marry Alec Graham.

The next morning, while Ben slept late, I filled Mom and Stephen in on everything Rafe told us.

"I'll call Father Mahon and find out where we are with Seers and Protectors. How did Rafe know that you are the first female Seer?"

"I have no idea. I didn't even know."

Stephen shrugged as he took a drink of his coffee. "It wasn't of any consequence, I thought. But now with Ben…."

When Stephen trailed off, Mom looked back and forth between the two of us. "What about Ben?"

I pulled Mom further from the kitchen doorway into the dining area and through the patio doors, out onto the cold wrap-around deck. "Mom, Kyle and I are pretty sure Ben is a Seer, like Dad."

"What? How do you know?"

"The neighbor's cat."

Mom met with a confused stare.

"Ben is letting the neighbor's cat in every night and putting her out in the morning before you get up. The cat you told me that died of old age. It's white and fluffy. She likes to watch the birds."

Mom placed her hand over her mouth. "Are you sure it's the same cat, Ainsley?"

"Yes. Kyle and I both petted her, and she was cold to the touch under all that fur. Kyle is the one who told me she was dead. As a Protector, he's more attuned to people and animals stuck between realms. And before you ask, we have no idea why animals are sometimes still here, but Kyle said they eventually disappear. It's creepy."

Mom turned to Stephen, who had joined us on the deck, the steam from his coffee quickly blowing over his cup. "Stephen, are you saying this Jai-ish is going to come after Ainsley *and* Ben?"

Stephen wrapped his free arm around Mom's shoulder. "We are doing everything we can to see where we stand, Stella. All of us would give up our lives for Ainsley and Ben. Trust me on this."

Mom hugged Stephen, but the look of uncertainty in his eyes sent a colder chill up my spine than even this North Carolina December morning.

"Stephen?"

He rolled his eyes over to me.

"You own a .308, don't you?"

He pulled away from the hug with Mom. "Yes. Why?"

"Alec told me that is what the shooter used to kill Mark Tahl."

"A .308? That would do quite a bit of damage."

I nodded. "It did," I whispered, seeing Tahl's final moments in the back of my mind. "You were still in Charleston the night Tahl died, right?"

"Ainsley, what are you asking?" Mom demanded, her eyes wide.

"That's all right, Stella," Stephen said. "I was home in Charleston when Kyle called me that night. Why on earth would you think I would commit murder?"

I shook my head. "I don't think you did. It was something Rafe Kae said last night. He said that Jai-ish might try to get to me by using someone I'm close to, someone I wouldn't suspect. The truth is, I would *never* suspect you, but you do own that same type of gun."

Stephen pulled me into a hug, and I felt Mom's hand as she rubbed my arm. "Ainsley, Jai-ish can't possess me. I'm a believer, remember. I belong to God, in this realm and the next."

~ ~ ~

I tried to slip out of the house alone to visit Kyle, but Ben was awake and insisted that he go with me to see his friend. Kyle had been like an older brother to Ben these last few years, so I finally relented. I couldn't very well say no to Ben.

When we walked into Kyle's hospital room, the doctor was leaning over his leg and checking on the small opening in the cast to ensure the stitches were not infected.

"Mr. Drekr, it appears you are healing well. How do you feel?"

"With all the painkillers you've got me on, I have no idea," Kyle answered with a celebrity smile. He'd ditched the hospital gown for a tee shirt and shorts that were easy to keep above the cast.

The doctor laughed. "Well, that is a blessing. I can lower these cables a bit to give your hip a rest, but we still need to keep it up and immobile."

"How long until I can walk? Maybe with a cane or something?" Kyle shifted uneasily in the bed, pushing himself up with his arms to change position slightly. "How long until I can work out again?"

The doctor shook his head. "It will still be a while. You will have to learn to stand again, mostly balancing on your good leg. Then we will work on the rehabilitation. Months, probably, Mr. Drekr. If you try to stand now, you're just going to fall and delay your recovery."

When the surgeon left, Ben walked to Kyle's side. "Wow, months. Sucks to be you."

"Shut up, kid," Kyle said and swatted at Ben but missed. They both laughed.

The two continued to talk about Ben's winter break, the girl he had been talking to at the gym, and Kyle's next move with Detective Wallace. I silently rolled my eyes but allowed the two to continue for at least a half-hour before deciding that I needed to talk with Kyle. Alone.

"Ben, why don't you run down to the gift shop and grab Kyle some candy," I said, handing Ben my debit card. "You know the PIN. Get yourself some too."

"Sounds good, Ains. What do you want, Kyle?"

Kyle rambled off some candy, and Ben went out the door.

I hurriedly sat down on the side of the bed opposite Kyle's casted leg. "Kyle, I need to tell you what happened last night with Judge Kae before Ben gets back."

Kyle listened to me as I told him everything revealed to us last night about Jai-ish.

"I'm sure there are other Seers and Protectors, Reynolds. I haven't worked with any, though. He said you're the first woman?"

"Yes. Stephen confirmed it."

Kyle reached for my hand and held it. "I knew it. I felt it yesterday. I told you that you are special. There is something about you that sets you apart from everyone else within the organization. Now we know."

"Is that what you wanted to tell me? Yesterday morning, it seemed like you were going to say something that would change our friendship."

Kyle frowned. "Like what?"

I shrugged. "I don't know. The way you were wording everything, I thought maybe you wanted...more."

"More what?"

"I don't know, Kyle!" I suddenly jumped up and away from him. The look on Kyle's face was pure shock and confusion. Apparently, I had read him wrong yesterday. "I thought maybe you wanted more from our friendship."

Kyle's mouth dropped open. "You're with Graham."

"I know. That's why I couldn't figure out what you were saying to me or why."

Kyle closed his mouth. It was a moment before he had himself together to answer. "Reynolds, what I tried to tell you yesterday morning was that after being with you for the last few years, *working* with you, I know you are something special. Come over here and sit down. For crying out loud, I can't chase you."

When I regained my seat on the bed, Kyle took my hand once more. "Whoever that demon was got in my head for just a moment the other day. For a split second, I saw myself kissing you. I mean really kissing you – and more – and I wanted that. I wanted you. But don't you see? That's how the demon was able to hurt me. It took my love for you and twisted it into something perverse. I do love you, but I am not in love with you. You are like a little sister to me. If anyone can make you happy and fulfilled, it's-"

"I know. Alec."

"I was going to say you. Only you can make yourself happy and fulfilled. Yeah, Alec Graham has a lot to do with how you love others, but loving yourself comes from you. Don't get confused. As your Protector, I will fight for you, but ultimately everything is up to you."

"Well, I love you too. You are my annoying older brother. And I am glad that you are not thinking about ravishing me on the hospital floor." I winked and kissed Kyle on the cheek.

Kyle's smirk grew, and he opened his mouth to say something when a high-piercing scream came from the hall.

"What was that?" I asked, pulling away from Kyle as I stood.

"A patient, maybe?"

The scream came again, and then a voice boomed through the hall and into Kyle's room. "Beacon! Where are you?" The scream came again.

"Reynolds! Don't!" Kyle shouted at me as I raced to the hospital room door. I eased it open to see thin Stacia in a hospital gown held with a scalpel against her neck by a man I had never seen before. He was tall and lanky with sores across his face, thinning blond hair that hung in wisps on his forehead. He had the twitchy look of a drug addict in his eyes.

"Ainsley, don't go out there," Kyle hissed at me from his bed.

I didn't look back at him. I just continued to watch the man and Stacia. The man's arm hooked around her throat, and as he squeezed, the scalpel ever so slightly pierced her skin. She screamed again.

"Beacon! Seer! Whatever name you are using now! Come out, or the girl dies!" Although the man appeared frail, his voice said otherwise.

"Jai-ish," I whispered.

"Ainsley, don't," Kyle pleaded. "For the love of God, do not go out there."

I looked back at Kyle over my shoulder. His clear blue eyes pleaded with me. I could see the tears behind them.

"He's going to kill her if I don't go."

"He's going to kill *you* if you do go."

We stared at each other as the man in the hall continued to call for me, and Stacia continued to scream.

Finally, I made the decision. "I'm sorry, Kyle. Tell my family I love them."

As I moved out into the hall, I heard Kyle shout my name and then a horrible thud behind me, but I refused to look back. The man with the scalpel smiled as he saw me.

"The one named Ainsley Reynolds," he seethed.

"Are you Jai-ish or another inferior copy?" I straightened my shoulders as I walked closer to the man, my nails digging into my palms. If I could just get him to let go of the girl, maybe I could expel the demon. I could hear the medical staff in their hiding places, crying and whispering to each other in panicked voices. *Stay calm, Ainsley.*

"What do you think?" the man snarled.

Suddenly, an image crossed my mind. It was definitely X-rated and included Alec and me. Yes, I had thought of Alec like that many, many times over the last four years. It was lust, and the demon was trying to use it against me.

"Is that the best you can do?" I asked, pushing the images out of my head. I wasn't going to let him trap me with those. God knew Alec and I planned to marry, and we hadn't done anything. I was still a virgin at twenty-two.

The man smiled before he kissed Stacia on the cheek and then pushed her to the ground. I saw my opening and raised my hand, but before I could say the words building inside me, another image jumped into my mind.

A disturbing image. An image of Kyle and me, most likely the same image the other demon had conjured up for Kyle. I tried to push it away, to see the man possessed by the demon, but I couldn't focus. Everywhere I looked, I saw Kyle and me. I squeezed my eyes shut to concentrate.

"Not real. Never happened."

"Hasn't happened yet, love," the man/demon said. "But you want it to happen. Deep down, you do."

I shook my head as I opened my eyes. However, my mouth wouldn't open. I tried to raise my hands to the man, but my body refused to obey. What was happening?

Suddenly, a pain shot through my back and into my chest. It moved across my ribcage and under my left arm. I wanted to scream, but there was no sound.

The pain intensified, and then it became hard to breathe. My body finally collapsed onto my knees, and I stared at the man standing not ten feet from me.

"I did think you were different. I should have known better, the way you dress for attention, practically begging for man's approval. I'm not even surprised to see you on your knees. You disappoint me." The man raised his hand, and I could almost feel his fingers wrapping around my heart as I slumped onto the floor. *He's killing me. God, please, no.*

I was losing focus as the hall began to melt away into darkness. Then there was an explosion of noise around me. I tried hard to hang on to the sound of the ding of the elevator and Ben's voice screaming, "Ains!" My vision narrowed further when I saw Kyle dragging himself across the floor from his room on his forearms. My vision was entirely black when I felt Kyle throw his 200-plus-pound body over mine and say something in Latin I couldn't make out, his arms wrapping tightly around me.

The last thing I heard was gunshots.

# CHAPTER TWELVE

I woke up in the hospital with various wires attached to me and a blood pressure cuff that I knew was bruising me every time it went off. I didn't move at first as I struggled to remember what had happened.

Jai-ish, or a demon pretending to be Jai-ish, called me out in the hospital hallway in front of Kyle's room. I'd gone to stop him, and at first, he had thrown images of Alec and me making love, but I had been able to push them away because I knew we hadn't done anything. Alec would one day be my husband if I lived.

I felt shame as I remembered what Jai-ish had shown me next. It was of Kyle and I having sex, *not* making love, but something out of an X-rated movie that you might accidentally run across at night on cable. Before I could push the image away, Jai-ish had started the process of stopping my heart. When I blacked out, I knew he was succeeding.

So, how was I alive now?

I quietly sat up in the bed. Alec was asleep in a chair with legs outstretched in front of him. He appeared worn out. He was wearing a pair of jeans and a thermal long-sleeve shirt. I could tell he hadn't shaved in a few days.

"Alec?" My voice was weak and hoarse, and a slight tremor of pain shot through my chest again. I took a deep breath, but it felt like I'd swallowed air as heavy pressure continued to build in my chest.

"Alec?"

Alec's eyes fluttered open, and he stared at me for a moment as if not sure if he was dreaming. I gave him a small smile.

That was all it took for him to rush over to the bed, moving the wires out of his way. "Hey, baby. You're awake. Take it easy." He lowered me back onto the pillow when I tried to sit up further. I watched as he pressed the call button.

"Yes?" a woman's voice came over the speaker.

"She's awake. I need someone in here." He said the words with such a commanding presence, I wanted to make a joke, but my mind wasn't fast enough.

"What happened? I should be dead."

Alec lowered his lids as he stared down at the bed, his jaw clenching.

"Alec, what is it?"

A doctor and a nurse both bustled in and moved between Alec and me as they began checking my vitals and fussing at my machines. I watched as Alec moved to the end of the room and started texting someone on his phone.

"Miss Reynolds, how do you feel?" the doctor, a blonde woman in her mid-to-late fifties, asked me.

"I'm not sure. What happened?"

The doctor frowned as if she wasn't sure how much to tell me. "We had an incident with a patient from another floor. You got caught in the middle, and apparently, you suffered a mild cardiac arrest."

"I had a heart attack?"

"A heart attack happens when blood stops flowing to the heart. A cardiac arrest is when your heart stops suddenly, usually with no real warning. Yours just tried to stop. You're going to have to take it easy while we try to figure out what brought this on."

"I heard gunshots before I passed out."

"It was the only way the police could stop the man from hurting anyone. He refused to drop the scalpel."

I blinked. Yes, that made sense. The police would have viewed him as a deranged patient and forcibly stopped him from hurting the medical staff and patients.

"What about my friend Kyle and my brother Ben? I heard both of them. How is the girl Stacia?"

The doctor glanced up at Alec as he approached the bed again. This time, his face didn't wear the relieved look it had when I woke up. He was sad.

"Ainsley," he said, taking my hand. "Ben is physically fine, although he is scared and worried about you. I messaged your mom. She, Stephen, and Ben are on their way. Stacia is a bit shaken up, but she'll be fine."

I nodded. When Alec didn't continue, I finally asked, "What about Kyle? I saw him pulling himself across the floor to protect me. He covered me with his own body. That's the last thing I remember."

Alec exchanged glances with the doctor, and then he sat down on the edge of my bed and leaned very close to my face, forcing me to look into his green eyes. "Kyle's heart stopped."

My eyes grew wide as I waited for him to finish his sentence.

Instead, he ran his hand up and down my arm.

"But?" I asked, prompting him to finish.

"There is no but, Ainsley. Kyle's heart stopped," he leaned down closer to whisper in my ear, so the doctor still standing at the foot of the bed couldn't hear. "His heart stopped in place of yours."

When he pulled away, my vision blurred. It took me a moment to realize the stinging heat in my eyes were tears. "Kyle is...dead?"

Alec nodded.

I opened my mouth to say something, but instead, I found myself gasping to take a breath. I couldn't breathe; I couldn't swallow. My throat was closing up. My mind swirled.

*Kyle couldn't be dead. He certainly did not fall onto the hospital floor and drag himself out into the hall to sacrifice himself for me. No! God, no! That couldn't have happened. He told me not to go out into the hall. He told me I would die. He wasn't supposed to die instead of me! This is my fault. Kyle is dead, and it is all my fault.*

I stared at Alec as he ran his hands over his head. I was gasping for air as the doctor barked orders, and a nurse rushed in and gave me a shot of something to calm me down. The doctor was asking Alec if I had a history of panic attacks.

Panic attacks. Cardiac arrest. Losing people. I had a history of a lot of things.

When the sedative kicked in, I cried myself to sleep with Alec running his fingers through my hair.

~ ~ ~

I didn't dream of Kyle. I didn't have a visitation. I didn't dream of anything, actually. The sedative just made me sleep.

When I woke again, Mom, Stephen, and Ben were in my room. Ben lunged for me as soon as he saw my eyes open. Although he was strangling me in his grip, I didn't complain. When he let me go, he held me by my shoulders, his dark eyes almost black. "I thought that man was going to kill you."

"I thought he had." My voice was weak again.

Mom gave me a hug next that lasted for a few minutes, then she neatly brushed my hair into a ponytail and secured it. When she moved away, Stephen gave me a hug as well as a quick kiss on the cheek.

"Where's Alec?"

"He had to go into the station. He said he would be back tonight to stay with you. You were very brave, Ainsley," Stephen said.

"Was I? I mean, really? Kyle is dead because of me. He told me not to go into the hall." My voice broke as I fought hard to keep the tears away.

Stephen sat down on the edge of the bed and carefully grasped the back of my neck, pulling my forehead against his, his dark beard lightly scratching my face the way Dad's used to when he was alive. "Alec and I watched the hospital's security camera footage. Kyle protected you with his dying breath. He chose to make his way into that hall. He disrupted Jai-ish's hold over you. He took the hit instead of you."

His eyes met mine. "Don't you dare make your life not worthy of his sacrifice. You would have done it for any of us."

I glanced quickly over at Ben, then back to Stephen. I whispered, "What happens now? Jai-ish is still out there somewhere. Will he come back when he realizes I didn't die?"

"You don't have to whisper. Stephen and Mom told me everything," Ben said.

Shock must have registered across my face because Ben approached my bed again. "I got off the elevator and saw the man standing above you with the scalpel and Kyle pulling himself on top of you to protect you. I'm not sure what happened next. I was so angry and scared that suddenly I saw everyone...differently."

"What do you mean?" My voice was coming out a whisper again.

"The man had this shadow around him that moved in and out, like a dark mist. You were on the floor, balled up on your side by this time. Kyle was on top of you saying something in another language, but you both had this enormous light seeping out from under you. It was so bright that for a second, I couldn't see you anymore. When the police shot the man, the dark mist vanished. Then I watched as Kyle's light began to fade. Then his light was just gone."

Mom, Stephen, and I looked at one another. We were all three crying.

Ben placed his hand on my shoulder. "Ains, your light flickered, but it never went out. I can still see it."

I covered his hand with mine. "You told Mom and Stephen this, and that's why they told you everything?"

He nodded.

Stephen, still sitting on the bed, reached across and patted Ben's arm. "I told him about his father and Kyle and you. Ben has inherited the gift, too but in a different form. Most likely, because of Gerald's abilities and yours, the combination is magnifying Ben's gift. I think he is seeing your soul."

"And you saw Kyle's light?" I asked weakly.

Ben nodded. "I saw it until he was gone. The staff told Mom that Kyle's heart stopped while he was on the floor, on you."

Ben had seen Kyle's soul until it left his body. Somehow that gave me some comfort. I knew I would see Kyle again one day, but it still hurt. It hurt to know that he was in an enormous amount of pain when he dropped to the floor from the height of his bed. It hurt to know that he couldn't stand, so he had dragged his heavily muscled body across his room and into the hall to try to help me. It hurt to know he had pushed himself on top of me and endured the pain to protect me and redirect Jai-ish's power from me to him.

I forced myself to take a deep breath. I could not allow my body to go into another panic attack. "So what happens now?"

Mom touched the blanket covering my feet. "We were discussing that. Perhaps it would be a good idea to get you out of town just until the Spring semester begins in late January. Alec said you could stay at his grandfather's place in South Carolina with Tilda and that girl, Stacia. I think the girl is supposed to go down with CPS and Alec in a couple of days."

"Leave Locklyn? Leave North Carolina? So, I'm just running from Jai-ish."

Stephen patted my arm. "We know what Judge Kae and Mark Tahl transcribed from their documents. You don't have a Protector anymore. If Jai-ish comes after you now, we don't have a plan."

I sat up a little straighter in the bed, forcing Stephen to move back. "Then we find another way. Doesn't Malus Navis have any Seers and Protectors besides Kyle and me? Rafe said we need an archangel. Is there a way to, I don't know, call one down or something?"

Stephen smiled. "I don't think archangels are that easy to summon."

"I'm not going to run away. Do you know what Jai-ish showed me? Do you know how he got in my head? The same way he got into Kyle's head. He showed me perverse images of Kyle and me having sex." I pointed at Ben, whose eyes were wide, and added, "Which we never, ever did. But it threw me so far off, just like it did Kyle, that it was easy for Jai-ish to overpower me this time."

I turned back to Stephen. "I need to double-check myself and make sure that there is nothing in my life that Jai-ish can use against me. He tried to use my relationship with Alec, but it didn't work. I have to block the images he projects somehow. I need you to find some more Seers and Protectors in the organization and get them here. And I *need* an archangel."

"I can help with that last demand," a deep voice said from the doorway. Rafe Kae stood with his back against the frame wearing his dapper three-piece suit and looking quite out-of-place in the sterile, barely decorated hospital room.

He stepped forward, surveying my family before his sapphire blue eyes landed on me. "I can help secure you an archangel. I can get you the one who faced Jai-ish a millennia ago."

~ ~ ~

I napped on and off the rest of the day. Mom, Stephen, and Ben left when Alec came in about the time the sky took on a pink and blue haze through the large window. Alec pulled a chair close to my bed, draped his arms across my lap, and rested his head on the stiff hospital blanket.

I ran my fingers through his hair. "Get anywhere on the case?"

"Not this one. I did manage to close two cases today and file the paperwork. Then I got a call from the lead homicide investigator in Charleston, South Carolina, asking for my input on another case. As for Mark Tahl, I'm starting to believe anyone could have pulled that trigger if Jai-ish possessed them. We haven't located the murder weapon."

"I think you're right."

Alec squeezed my legs before pushing himself away from my lap and closer to my face. He leaned on his elbows. "How are you feeling?"

"Weak. Tired. Deeply sad. All the things."

He tucked a loose lock of my hair behind my ear. "We'll figure this out, baby. I promise," he whispered.

"Ainsley?" came a small voice from the doorway.

Stacia stood just inside my room, wearing a hospital gown with another one over it like a robe, her dark hair pulled into a ponytail.

Alec moved off his seat in a flash. "Hey Stacia, how are you feeling? Here, come take this chair."

The girl smiled apologetically at Alec before she slid into the chair next to my bed.

"Are you okay, Stacia?" I asked.

She nodded her head. "I'm sorry about your friend."

I placed my hand with the IV still taped to the top over Stacia's thin one. "Me, too. He was a good guy."

"That man came into my room and pulled me from the bed. It all happened so fast."

"You're safe now," Alec said as he pulled the recliner chair up to the opposite side of the bed.

I glanced at Alec. Was Stacia safe? Were any of us safe with a high-level demon who could possess almost anyone roaming around? I patted Stacia's hand again. "You're safe now," I repeated his words as hollow as they sounded.

Stacia's eyes glazed over as she leaned heavily on the edge of the bed. "It was so scary. After the man let me go, and I saw you drop to the floor, I was terrified. Your face turned white, and you were gasping for air."

I swallowed hard.

"When your friend crawled out there, he kept saying something I couldn't understand over and over, except for the last thing. I understood the last sentence before he…you know."

I blinked back the tears as I patted her hand again. "What did he say?"

Tears began falling silently down Stacia's cheeks. "He said, *I love you, Ainsley Reynolds.*"

Stacia suddenly lunged at me, and I realized she was hugging me and sobbing. I wrapped my arms around her and let her cry. Silent tears were streaming down my face too and into her hair.

Alec sat back in the recliner with his eyes shut, his hands covering his mouth. I knew what he was thinking. Kyle sacrificed his life for mine. It was just like Jesus said. There was no greater love than to lay down one's life for his friends.

~ ~ ~

After Stacia had let all of her emotions out, she slumped back down in the chair. "I'm sorry. It's just so sad. I've never seen anyone love like that before."

"Don't be sorry. Kyle loved his friends deeply," I answered, trying to keep my voice steady. What I wanted to do was roll over and cry myself to sleep. What stopped me was that I had a feeling Stacia needed us in this moment. She was reaching out.

"Were you two together?" Stacia hesitantly asked as she looked over at Alec. His expression was unreadable.

I shook my head. "No, Kyle and I are – um, *were* – just really close friends. He was like a brother to me."

"I don't have any brothers or sisters. I couldn't imagine someone doing that for me. His death is all over the news."

"The news?"

Alec cleared his throat. "Stephen notified Kyle's mother and his investigative crew about his death. Don't worry. I already talked to security. They're keeping the media out of the hospital." When I raised my brows, he added, "The report is that Kyle's heart stopped due to an underlying condition."

*Underlying condition.*

Somewhere in my mind, I'd forgotten how well-known Kyle was internationally due to his show. To me, he'd always just been Kyle. Infuriating, annoying, big-brotherly, joking Kyle. I wiped my eyes.

*I had loved him.*

Alec squeezed my hand. "I'm going down to the cafeteria for some coffee. Can I get you anything?"

I managed a smile as I shook my head.

"Stacia, do you want anything? My treat."

Stacia's hollow eyes studied Alec for a moment, then shyly, she asked, "Do you think I could get a Pepsi and some Twizzlers?"

Alec smiled. "I think that can be arranged. I'll be right back."

"He's nice," Stacia commented after Alec had left the room. "Is he your boyfriend?"

"Yes, on both counts." I shifted in the bed. I was beginning to feel tired, but I didn't want Stacia to leave either. "Tell me about school."

"There's nothing to tell. I'm hoping to get a college scholarship."

"What about your friends?"

"I don't have a lot of those."

"My brother Ben is in seventh grade at the year-round school, Calabria. Do you know him?"

"No, I don't think so. I mean, I saw him in the hall today with your mother."

"Depending on how I feel, I would like to ride along with Alec to South Carolina when you leave to meet Tilda. She's fantastic. You will love her. Maybe I can ask Ben to come since he's so close to your age."

"Okay. Um, Ainsley, can I tell you something?"

"Sure, Stacia," I answered, leaning my head back on the pillows. The act of conversing was quickly draining me.

"I saw you with your family, and you look so close. I don't have that. I'm afraid if I go to Detective Graham's house and stay with Tilda that it might hurt too much to leave." She lowered her eyes. "I don't want to get hurt."

I reached for Stacia's hand and squeezed. "I know. I'm going to pray about this, and we're going to give this over to God." I waited until she raised her gaze to meet mine. "I believe there is a reason God brought you into my life, into Alec's life. I think it has to do with surrounding you with believers in the Christian faith for protection. To move your life onto a certain path and to get you closer to people who can help you find your purpose."

I laid back again and closed my eyes. I was so tired.

"Ainsley? Can you tell me about this faith you and your family have?"

I opened my eyes to see Stacia's dark eyes watching me. There was a glimmer of hope in them.

*Always be ready to share your hope in Jesus Christ.* The words I had heard Stephen preach from the Book of 1st Peter echoed through my head.

"Yes, of course, Stacia. Bring your chair a little closer and grab my Bible from the table. See the tabs on the side? Let's start in the Book of John."

# CHAPTER THIRTEEN

Although the doctors were worried about me and Alec argued with me in the hospital room so loudly that the hospital staff threatened to throw him out, I was released the following day to go home. My physician made me sign a release form and cautioned me that if I got another pain in my chest to immediately call an ambulance if I didn't drop dead first. Jai-ish had done some damage to the heart muscle. I'd thanked the doctor calmly for her advice and then went into the bathroom and shut the door to dress, leaving Alec to handle the new prescription medication for my heart.

I'd silently cried with my back against the shower wall so Alec couldn't hear me in the next room over the water. I was terrified to face Jai-ish again, but I was not going to let Kyle's death be in vain.

I couldn't.

Alec drove me home in silence and then walked me to my room. Then per our relationship, we argued loudly about whether I should stay in Locklyn at Mom's house or permanently escape to his estate in South Carolina. Mom stormed in once and bawled us both out for shouting, saying it wasn't good for my heart. It took everything I had not to make the smart-alec comment that if I faced Jai-ish unprepared again, then it wouldn't matter. That would've only sent her into a worrisome spiral, and Alec probably would have tossed me into his SUV and dumped me off on Tilda's front porch.

When Mom left my room, Alec walked to the window and placed his hands behind his head.

"What is wrong with you?" I asked, sitting down on the edge of the bed.

"What is wrong with me?" He whirled around, this time keeping his voice low. "Oh, I don't know, Ainsley. Let me count the ways. A demon is trying to kill my girlfriend. I still haven't found Mark Tahl's killer. Kyle Drekr is dead, and we still need to make arrangements to get his body back to L.A. My girlfriend is hellbent on facing this demon as soon as she can build an army. Oh! And I have to figure out what Rafe Kae is up to when he says he is going to secure us an archangel."

Alec stood above me with his hands on his hips, his face blood red. Then, just as suddenly as his outburst, I watched as his clenched jaw softened and his features crumpled. He dropped to his knees in front of me beside the bed and placed his head on my lap. His hands clutched my lower body as he laid there, seemingly defeated.

"I think my own heart stopped when your mother called and told me what happened, that you were unconscious, and that Kyle was dead. I don't know what I would do without you. I missed four years of your life, and now that I have you back, it's unimaginable to think you might disappear."

I ran my fingers through his short hair while he continued, "I know you and Kyle were close. Sometimes I was jealous of your relationship, the way you confided in him. Even in South Carolina, when the two of you couldn't stand to be in the same room with each other, there was a tension. The two of you hurled insults at each other the way others yell *I love you*. The evening that I saw you in Kyle's hotel room and he had his shirt off…well, you know how that turned out. I felt that jealousy rearing its head the other day when I overheard the two of you talking, and I knew in the pit of my stomach that if Kyle confessed that he was in love with you, I would lose you forever."

With that last statement, I moved my hand from the top of Alec's head to his chin and forced him to lift his head and look at me. "Alec, Kyle told me that he loved me like a little sister and that he was not in love with me. He said I was special in what I can do as a Seer. Alec, even if Kyle had told me something else, that wouldn't have changed how I feel about you. I love you so much. So much that Jai-ish tried to use my feelings for you against me, and it didn't work."

I placed both my hands on the sides of Alec's face as he leaned in and kissed me. As we kissed, I could sense our emotions heightening, the sweet kiss becoming urgent. Alec pulled himself up and onto the bed as I laid back. It felt nice to be in his arms, safe, the scent of his cologne surrounding me; apples and cinnamon and a hint of sandalwood, probably from the bottle of Hugo Boss I'd seen on his bedroom dresser a few days ago.

Alec pushed himself up and removed his shirt with one quick motion. I ran my hand over Alec's defined chest and ab muscles, then I pulled him back down onto the bed with me. I never wanted to lose Alec again, and I could feel his urgent need not to lose me either.

Suddenly, the images from Jai-ish flashed through my mind. With some reluctance, I placed my hand on

Alec's hard chest and pushed. He immediately stopped kissing me.

"Okay, we have to stop," I said, struggling to catch my breath. "This is exactly what Jai-ish wants me to give in to."

"What?"

I looked Alec in the eye as I rubbed my finger across the stubble on his jaw. "Sex with you. He's looking for a weakness, a vice."

Alec pushed himself up onto his hands, straddling me, so he could see me better and place a few inches between us. "First off, I would never have sex with you in your mother's house."

I eyeballed the rumpled shirt beside me and raised my eyes to Alec's. He swiped the shirt off the bed.

"Second, why is he using sexual attraction to reveal your weakness?"

I shrugged. "He kept projecting images of us together to try to throw me off, but it didn't work."

Alec slowly moved off me, off the bed. "Tell me about the images." His tone of voice had changed into Detective Graham's voice as he pulled his shirt back on.

"I am not going to share those images with you until after you have proposed to me, married me, and we are on our honeymoon," I answered back, pushing myself up onto my elbows.

Detective Graham continued studying my face.

I sighed. "Fine. Just things that had crossed my mind in the past. I've always thought about you. Jai-ish just rooted them out, that's all."

Alec's eyes narrowed, and suddenly my throat felt dry. "Stephen told me what you said about how Jai-ish got to Kyle, how he ultimately got to you." His voice was quiet, as if some lightbulb was going off in his head.

Silently, I was sending hateful telepathic messages to Stephen. In what way was it necessary for Stephen to tell Alec, of all people, about the images of Kyle and me?

I swallowed. "It was just another one of Jai-ish's tricks."

Alec moved farther away from the bed. "But from what you just said about the images of you and me, they were imaginary scenarios *you* created."

I started to speak, but Alec held up his hand. "I can understand that. I have an imagination, especially when it comes to you. But, Ainsley, did Jai-ish show you images of you and Kyle that *you* made up at some point? Did he show Kyle images that Kyle himself had imagined? Of the two of you together?" He practically spit out the last question.

I sat up on the bed. I opened my mouth and then quickly closed it. Maybe. Perhaps once, I'd thought about Kyle like that. For a fleeting moment. I couldn't even entertain the thought of why I would have, though. Kyle and I were close, and over the last few years, we had joked and bantered back and forth, and sometimes, flirted. But it had been harmless. I looked back up at Alec, who was watching me intently. He was a detective. If I lied to him, he would see the lie cross my face. If I told him that I had thought of Kyle like that at some point, Alec might walk away from me. Again.

"I can't speak for Kyle," I said. "He didn't tell me explicitly what Jai-ish showed him, but he did say that he found it disturbing."

One of Alec's narrowed eyes twitched.

"And of what you saw?" His voice was raspy now, his jaw clenching, anger building behind his eyes.

"I never had sex with Kyle."

Alec exhaled. "But you thought about it. That's how Jai-ish got in your head." He started for the door.

"No," I said with more force than I expected. Alec stopped with his back to me, his hand on the doorknob.

"No," I repeated, lowering my voice. "If I did imagine one night with Kyle, then it was years ago after you left. I hadn't thought about that at all. I've never slept with anyone. If Kyle did ever envision us together at some point, I don't believe it was recent. But it didn't matter. The visions were enough to render us powerless against Jai-ish. Alec, I love you. You are the only one I want. The only man I want to spend the rest of my life with. Don't walk away from me for something that flittered through my head once. If I were to judge you on where your imagination roams, what would happen then?"

Alec turned to look at me, his eyes fiery, a tiny grin slowly growing across his mouth. "I probably wouldn't stand a chance against Jai-ish either. Especially when it came to you."

He started towards me, but I held my hand up this time. "I need to purge myself of anything and everything unclean in my head before I face Jai-ish again. I have to take every thought captive. You are a temptation."

"Oh?" Alec gave me a quick kiss on the mouth before starting for the door again. "Well, then, I'd better stay out of your way and see if I can help round up some Seers and Protectors."

"Well, don't forget I'm riding down to Mire Marsh with you when you take Stacia to meet Tilda."

Alec waved me off in dismissal as he retreated down the hall toward the living room.

"I mean it, Alec. I'm going!"

~ ~ ~

Father Mahon arrived from New York with only one Seer and one Protector that evening. Maren Bell showed up less than an hour later. All of us were quiet at first in honor of Kyle. The priest said he had contacted Kyle's mother in Los Angeles, and together they had made arrangements for his body to ship home. The television networks were running tributes for Kyle, showing some of his most popular shows. I couldn't bear to watch them.

Alec ordered a large amount of food from a local barbeque place for delivery, and then we all scattered about the living room and dining area to discuss our options, if any, with a demon like Jai-ish.

"Is Judge Kae coming?" Stephen asked Alec.

"I don't know. I texted him earlier about the meeting. I haven't heard back."

Stephen frowned. "I wish he would tell us how he plans to call on this archangel."

Father Mahon took a sip of the dark roast coffee Mom had made him. "Tell me about this judge."

I listened as Stephen and Alec filled Father Mahon in on what they knew about Rafe. My mind wandered to Kyle's last moments, and I had to pull it back. It would do me no good to get upset now.

The Seer who accompanied Father Mahon was a young man named Robert, tall with curly black hair. His Protector was another man who looked vaguely familiar, but I couldn't place him. He was older than the Seer, probably in his late forties or early fifties, with brown hair and a weathered face. Every once in a while, he would look over at me.

When the food arrived, Mom and I set everything up on the kitchen counter banquet style. Alec had ordered enough food for a horde of people. We had pulled-pork barbecue, french fries, baked beans, coleslaw, warm hamburger buns, pretzel buns, and apple crisp. The items were in large aluminum foil pans, and there were multiple pans of each. I waited until everyone made their plate before making mine. Then I started to settle myself in front of Alec, who had pulled a dining room chair into the living room but decided to sit near the Protector instead. I lowered myself neatly beside his legs.

The man glanced down at me as I smiled up at him.

"You've grown up," he remarked, his voice husky like my father's. A little ping hit my heart.

"I guess so. You look familiar. Have I met you before?"

The man half-smiled and nodded his head. "A long time ago. You were probably ten or eleven. It was right before your father met Kyle Drekr. Gerald was requested to investigate a case involving someone poisoning groups of people. Think anthrax."

"Oh," I said. "So, you worked with my father? I didn't catch your name."

Upon hearing that, Ben came over and scooted in next to me, balancing his plate with one hand.

"My name is Finn McCallister. I worked with your father on that one case. He was a very gifted man. I was saddened when I learned of his death. There are more Seers in the world, but either they keep their gift to themselves, or we don't know about them."

"How did I meet you?" I asked.

"After we finished the case, your father rushed back here to be with you and your baby brother while your mother attended a writer's conference somewhere. Your father and I had hit it off and wanted to continue talking about what we had learned from each other. I stayed at a nearby motel, and the four of us," he waved his hand to include Ben and me, "had lunch out twice."

"What exactly does a Seer and Protector do? I mean, how does it work?" Ben asked.

Finn patted Ben on the shoulder. "Don't worry, my boy. Robert and I are going to go over everything with you. The remarkable thing is you already have so much in you that instinctively I believe you know what to do."

"What do you mean?"

Finn looked over at Stephen, who set his can of Dr. Pepper down on the end table to answer Ben.

"Ben, Alec and I viewed the hospital's cameras. You are the reason Kyle was successful in saving Ainsley. When you came off that elevator, the shock and fear, and even anger, combined with Kyle's abilities, is what diverted Jai-ish's power away from Ainsley."

Ben's face went white as a sheet. I knew what he was thinking. I set my plate of food on the floor and grabbed Ben's shoulders.

"No, you did not kill Kyle. Jai-ish would have killed both of us if it hadn't been for you. Kyle wasn't strong enough to completely protect me."

Ben's dark eyes met mine. He nodded once, letting me know I could let go of his shoulders now.

I glanced back up at Stephen. "So, what now?"

Father Mahon cleared his throat. "I have a theory, but I would like to speak to this Judge Kae first."

"He still hasn't returned my last call or text. Tell us what you are thinking," Alec said, placing his plate on the floor in front of him, clearly ready to get to work.

The priest scooted closer to the edge of the couch. "We channel Robert and Finn's abilities into Ainsley and Ben. This should magnify both Seers' powers and allow them to banish Jai-ish. Along as there is nothing Jai-ish can use against them."

Alec and I exchanged glances. "Father Mahon, won't channeling their power leave them exposed? Won't we need a Protector?" I asked.

Finn cleared his throat. "Ainsley, Robert and I will still be there. It won't be all of our abilities, but enough. It doesn't matter anyway. Jai-ish wants you. We are willing to die if that's what it takes to expel that demon for a thousand years."

I looked over at Robert. The young man was staring down at the plate of uneaten food on his lap. Finn followed my gaze.

"Aren't we, Robert?"

Robert looked up and nodded, his face solemn. *Yeah, right.*

I peered over at Stephen and Alec. Maybe I could channel Robert's and Finn's abilities. Maybe not.

"Is it possible for me to channel Robert's, Finn's, and Ben's abilities while they stay hidden?"

"Take on Jai-ish by yourself?" Father Mahon sounded incredulous.

"Not by myself. I would have the power of two Seers and a Protector as well as my own."

Father Mahon squinted his eyes at me. Everyone quieted in the room.

"Ainsley, we already lost Kyle Drekr, one of the most talented Protectors. Sending you out on your own, *hoping* that the Seers' powers will stay with you without them actually present, is not a risk we should take."

My stare never wavered from the priest's eyes. "I don't want Ben present."

"Ains, it's fine," Ben said, sinking his chin into my shoulder.

"It's not fine, Ben. You haven't even laid eyes on a demon yet, a Muladach. Jai-ish is a higher-level demon that works outside of the Muladach's rules. He can move between realms by his own free will. He can possess humans. At this rate, we might never find out who shot Mark Tahl because it was probably someone Jai-ish possessed just long enough to pull the trigger."

My anger and frustration grew, and I quickly stood with my plate and headed for the kitchen. A few seconds later, Alec joined me at the counter, his eyebrow raised in my direction.

"If you're done throwing a tantrum," he whispered, "you need to rejoin us in the living room."

I practically growled at him. "Come outside with me." I drug him out through the patio doors onto the back deck. After I slid the door shut, I braced myself against the cold wind in my leggings and sweatshirt. I walked to the end of the deck, so the people inside hopefully couldn't hear.

"This meeting is solving nothing!" I yelled, frustration fueling my anger.

"Your tantrum solves nothing!" he yelled back.

"I don't want Ben anywhere near Jai-ish. Even if he is more powerful than all the Seers, all the Beacons, I don't want him there!"

Alec walked toward me, his face so full of fury that I had to remind myself not to back down. He stopped just inches from me, and when he spoke, his voice was so low, I struggled to hear it over the wind. "*None* of this is about you. This is bigger than you or me, bigger than any of those people in your house. Your father knew that." He touched my shoulder, the wind whipping my hair around his hand. "Kyle knew that. Kyle knew the sacrifice was greater than him, so he made it without hesitation."

"I know he did," I whispered just loud enough for him to hear, my eyes filling with tears. "I know I can banish Jai-ish, but I'm scared, Alec. I'm terrified."

With that, I buried my face in Alec's shoulder and cried.

~  ~  ~

The next day, Alec, Ben, and I made the drive to Mire Marsh, South Carolina, arriving only thirty minutes before the social worker, Ms. Sears, and Stacia. The impressive house was still the same with its columns and neat landscape. Tilda had decorated the entire house for Christmas with wreaths half the size of my body and a twelve-foot tree in the foyer that only professional decorators could have set up.

I'd barely taken a step inside when the woman with the white bob pulled me into a hug.

"Ainsley! I am so happy to see you again! I knew my Alec made a mistake when he wasn't with you." She stepped away briefly, only to grab Alec into a hug.

"Thanks, Tilda," Alec answered as he gave her a sweet kiss on the cheek.

"Well, it's true. You were, I don't know the right word, disgruntled, maybe? Grumpy?"

"You were grumpy for four years without me?" I handed Alec the large drawstring sack of wrapped presents we'd brought to set under the enormous Christmas tree for Tilda and Stacia.

"Tilda's exaggeratin'," he answered, showing more of his Southern accent. It was thicker when he was around Tilda. "I wasn't grumpy the entire four years."

"That's right," Tilda said, smiling. "Sometimes, he was just depressed. Now! Where is this girl Stacia? And who do we have here?"

"This is my brother Benjamin."

Tilda wrapped her arms around a speechless Ben. I stifled a giggle. "That's right. Alec said you were comin' too. Well, you are a handsome fella, aren't you? I have a room made up for you and another one for your sister. And where is Stacia? I'm excited to meet her."

"They should be here any minute. Did you have any problems getting things ready?" Alec asked.

"No. I used the same decorator who does our Christmas decorations and lights to add some pizazz to the Cream Room."

"What's the Cream Room?" I asked, almost laughing at the title.

"Oh! Come with me, Ainsley! I'll show you."

Alec and a speechless Ben stayed in the foyer as I followed Tilda through the great hall and under an arched doorway into another smaller hall with two doors and a wooden staircase.

"Wow."

Tilda turned a bit as she ascended the stairs to walk alongside me. "All this is original. Ed and his family kept the maintenance up on the house. She's a real beauty."

On the second floor, Tilda stopped at the last of three doors on the right. "Here it is. The Cream Room." She swung the door open to reveal a spacious room with at least a ten-foot ceiling, cream-colored walls, and matching hand-carved moldings around the doorframe. An ornate ceiling fan swung lazily above a cream-colored wooden bed with a pale pink bed set. I opened a pair of double doors to an empty walk-in closet.

"Oh, don't worry. Once I get Stacia settled, I'll take her clothes shoppin'. It'll be so nice to have a girl to spoil."

"And spoiled she'll be," I answered and smiled. I poked my head into the attached bath and let out a little gasp. It contained a marble double-sink vanity, a toilet, a clawfoot bathtub, and a marble walk-in shower.

"Is that a *chandelier* in the bathroom?"

Tilda glanced up at the pink chandelier above the tub in the middle of the room. "Well, it's a tiny one. I thought she'd like it, so I had them take out the original one. Do you think it's too much?"

I shook my head. "No, I think it's perfect, Tilda. Stacia is going to love it. I know I do."

Tilda wrapped her arm around my waist, her head only as high as my shoulder. "Come on, dear, let's go downstairs and wait for her. You know, I'm willin' to spoil great-grandbabies too."

I laughed. "I bet you are, but Alec and I aren't even engaged yet."

As soon as we stepped back into the foyer, Tilda began fussing at Alec about popping the question until Ms. Sears arrived with Stacia. He answered Tilda's words with a patient *No, Ma'am* or *Yes, Ma'am*. It was the sweetest exchange I'd ever seen. Tilda wasn't Alec's blood relative, but she was every bit the grandmother he needed.

When Stacia walked in, Tilda smiled at her as if she was her long-lost daughter come home. I followed Tilda, Stacia, and Ms. Sears as they toured the house together to make sure it was everything CPS required in a foster home. Within two hours, Ms. Sears was satisfied with Stacia's arrangements and left to begin her journey back to Locklyn.

The five of us stood in the massive oak kitchen drinking glasses of sweet tea and eating Tilda's homemade lemon cookies.

"So, are you going to do virtual school through the county while you're here?" Ben asked Stacia.

"That's what Ms. Sears said."

"One of my friends does virtual. I can help get you set up before we leave in the morning. If you want."

"That would be great, Ben," Stacia answered, taking a sip of her tea. She could barely make eye contact with him. She was shy.

"Did you see my room?" Stacia asked me.

"Yes, I did," I answered, my eyes growing as big as hers. "Did you see your bathroom chandelier?"

Stacia nodded, and a little smile broke out across her face.

"Ainsley, you're welcome to stay here for as long as you like. We have plenty of rooms. Alec's old bedroom is ready too."

I playfully shouldered Alec. "What does your childhood bedroom look like?"

He smiled before popping the last bite of the cookie into his mouth. "I don't stay in that room anymore. It's decorated in Mighty Morphin Power Rangers at one end and posters of Britney Spears and The Phantom Menace on the other."

Stacia, Ben, and I laughed until we had tears in our eyes. Finally, Alec wrapped his arm around my waist and pulled me closer. "Anyway, I'm saving that room for a nursery one day."

"Oh? I hope you and your wife will be very happy."

Alec rolled his eyes as he slipped his arm away from me. "Come on, Ben. Let me show you where you're sleeping tonight. You get a room with a balcony."

~ ~ ~

The next morning, I made my way to the kitchen and brewed a pot of coffee for everyone before taking my cup back upstairs to the balcony off the second-floor hall. This balcony overlooked the grounds in front of the house. I was exhausted, and truth be told, my chest ached a little. I'd managed to forget about everything last night when Tilda invited me to go shopping with Stacia and her. I'd had so much fun dressing Stacia up that I could barely eat dinner before collapsing into the queen-size bed in one of the guest rooms on the second floor.

I'd just settled into a white rocker when Alec, fresh from the shower, joined me wearing jeans and a tee-shirt.

I pulled my hair up into a ponytail. "If I'd known you were going to come out here, I would have brought you a cup. I made coffee."

He gave me a quick kiss on the lips before sitting down in another rocker. "I'll get some when I go down. Thanks."

"It's not as chilly as I thought it would be this morning. I mean, for December." I was comfortable in just a pair of jeans, a long-sleeve thermal, and a chunky cardigan.

"Not yet. I think the high today is supposed to be 61 degrees." He took a deep breath of the cool air. "I think Ben and Stacia hit it off last night."

"Really? How do you know?"

"They woke me up at 3am giggling in Stacia's room."

My eyes grew wide.

Alec smiled. "Calm down, Big Sis. I opened the door and checked. They were sitting on the floor, watching a movie on Ben's laptop. I told them to finish the movie, then get to bed. I reminded Ben that we have a long day once we get back to Locklyn."

I sighed. "I wish I could leave Ben here. Keep him away from all of this."

Alec didn't answer. He was chewing on his lower lip and looking out at the landscape.

"What are you thinking?" I asked him.

A tiny smile threatened to break out on his face. "I was thinking that if we live through this, then one day, we can make this *our* home."

I turned my head before he could see the fear in my eyes. It wasn't if *we* lived through this. It was if *I* lived through it, me and whatever Seers and Protectors I could draw from during an attack.

Two hours later, we were in Alec's SUV headed back to Locklyn to meet with Stephen and the others from Malus Navis. We'd enjoyed an amazing breakfast made by Tilda and talked and laughed about everything under the sun. Tilda hugged each of us equally hard when we left, telling us how much she would miss us. Ben gave Stacia his phone number, and Alec asked Tilda to call and add a line to the cell phone plan for Stacia. The company could overnight a phone to her.

"Stacia is pretty cool," Ben said as he got comfortable in the back seat.

"I think so too," I agreed. "She's had a hard life. She needs this time with Tilda."

"Yeah, she told me some stories about her childhood. Pretty messed up," he answered.

Alec and I exchanged looks but didn't say anything. Ms. Sears had told Alec privately that if everything worked out with Tilda fostering Stacia, there was an excellent chance that Stacia could become a permanent member of the family over the next year. Stacia would mourn the loss of her biological family, but I felt that she would have a better – and safer – life with Tilda. Of course, Alec agreed he would ensure that if adoption were possible for Stacia, he would be listed as her guardian if anything should happen to the seventy-one-year-old woman.

I sent a silent prayer to God about Stacia and Tilda. They needed each other.

Alec turned an audiobook on, but it wasn't something I liked, so I slipped my earbuds in and turned the music up on my phone. Hours passed before Ben started getting insistent that we should stop to eat.

"I'm starving to death back here," Ben complained for the fortieth time.

"We left Tilda's not three hours ago," I answered him again for the fortieth time.

"I'm a teenager, Ains. I'm starving all the time."

Alec sighed. "All right. Next exit, and we will stop to get something to eat. We still have almost two hours to go before we get to Locklyn. Frankly, I'm starving too."

I squeezed Alec's bicep. "Must be all the muscle mass."

Ben groaned in the backseat. "You two are as bad as Mom and Stephen."

~  ~  ~

We pulled into the parking lot of a fast-food restaurant and decided to eat inside so we could take the opportunity for a restroom break. Ben and I had never taken a road trip together without Mom, so I had to admit, I was enjoying my rapidly-growing little brother.

Plus, since the loss of Kyle, I figured he and I both needed this time away. Kyle had been a big brother to Ben too.

Once we'd eaten and Ben's stomach was temporarily satisfied, we started back out to the truck. However, with a force I'd never felt before, the blacktop surged at me, and I lost my balance, landing on the cold asphalt.

"Ains, you okay?" Ben asked as he and Alec helped me up.

"Yeah," I mumbled as I tried to listen. There was a faint growling beyond the veil separating us from the other realm. The demons were here. Why? No sooner had I questioned this than the air rippled, knocking my equilibrium off again. This time Alec caught me before I landed on the ground.

"What is it?" he asked.

"There are demons here. There is at least one on the other side, moving back and forth. Right here." I touched the air in front of me. The vibration moved up my arm and into my chest. "There you are," I whispered.

"I don't see anything," Ben said.

"I don't either. I just feel it."

"Am I supposed to feel something too?" he asked.

"Probably not yet. This is a portal to the other realm." I scanned the area. "In a parking lot of all places."

"It wasn't always a parking lot," Alec added. "The area is old, and I'm pretty sure the North and South fought on this land. Could that kind of bloodshed create a portal?"

"Maybe, I'd have to ask-" I almost finished the sentence with *Kyle. I'd have to ask Kyle.* I took a deep breath. "I'd have to ask Father Mahon or Finn. Come on. We should go."

Alec and I started toward the truck, but Ben stood staring into the invisible spot of air. "Shouldn't we do something about it? The demon?"

"It hasn't moved into this realm yet. Even if it does, if I banish it, then my soul will light up like a flare. I might as well nail myself to a billboard and announce to Jai-ish that I'm here. That you're here."

Ben stared at me, and for a moment, his dark eyes reflected Dad's look of concern. "What if it comes through after we leave? What if it influences someone to murder?"

I studied my younger brother. He'd only known about Seers, Protectors, and discernment for a little while, yet here he was, willing to risk exposing us to save people he didn't know.

Just like Dad.

I dropped my gaze to the blacktop, slightly ashamed, torn between wanting to stand and fight Jai-ish and wanting to hide to stay alive. I almost died last time. Kyle *did* die.

"We'll give it a few minutes to see if it comes through."

*God, please, I don't know what to do.*

The three of us stood in the parking lot for at least fifteen minutes, the air growing colder. The air still rippled, but I managed to stay rooted to the ground. I could still hear the growling, although I said nothing to Ben or Alec. The snarls and hollow-sounding barks were getting louder. The Muladach was going to come through the portal soon.

With the next wave of energy came a burst of light, and I shielded my eyes as a demon leaped into this realm, landing on all fours. It sniffed the air, and then its reflective eyes landed on me. This one was like the others, heavily muscled with silvery transparent skin that revealed its organs beneath. It opened its gargoyle-like mouth to give me a glimpse of razor-sharp teeth.

I heard Ben gasp.

"What do you see?" I asked him.

"A black mist just materialized near you."

I pointed to the demon. "To Hell with you, Demon. You do not belong in this realm. You will not hurt these people, God's creations. Now go in Jesus' name!"

The Muladach snarled at me as it looked from me to Ben, a frothy substance dripping onto the blacktop. Then it leaned back onto its haunches, gave a bark, and disappeared.

"The mist is gone," Ben said.

"It was a demon, what we call a Muladach. You couldn't see it in its true form yet, but one day you will."

"Your soul did light up like a searchlight. You banished the Muladach?"

"Yes."

"Seems easy enough." Ben started for the truck.

"It's not," I called after him. "You have to believe completely that God's power flows through you. You have to become less."

Ben turned around at the truck door and shrugged. "I got it, Ains. Less of me, more of Him."

Frustration surged through me. How could he sound so flippant about it, like it was nothing to face demons? I'd struggled for four years with my identity as a Seer, my identity as a Believer, and here stood my younger brother as if watching a tutorial on YouTube about banishing demons.

As Ben climbed into the SUV, I started after him, but Alec put his hand on my arm.

"What?" I snapped.

"Hey, he's thirteen," Alec whispered. "He understands, but he wants to be brave for you. Father Mahon said Ben's showing both Seer and Protector abilities, plus new ones. He's trying to fill some very large shoes left by your father and Kyle. Give him time."

I blinked back tears. "I banished a demon, Alec. Time is something we no longer have."

# CHAPTER FOURTEEN

Three days later, hardly any of us had left the house. Finn and Robert, along with Stephen and Father Mahon, shared everything they could with Ben. One evening, I pulled Ben into my room and shared with him Dad's journal – the journal he'd made for me after discovering I had Seer abilities. Unfortunately, Dad hadn't lived long enough to give it to me himself.

I explained the rules of a Seer and Protector and cautioned Ben against breaking the rules. I shared with him my own painful consequences of breaking those rules before with Kyle.

Ben read the rules aloud, memorizing them:

*Rule Number One: Never communicate with the dead.*

*Rule Number Two: Never open yourself up and allow a demon to use you.*

*Rule Number Three: Never pass through to the other realm unless it is to save a soul.*

Of course, Ben had a ton of questions for me about these rules since Kyle had been a well-known paranormal investigator whose livelihood depended on him being able to interact with the dead. I told Ben about my trip to the Ashbury Estate in South Carolina with Stephen, Alec, and Kyle. I told him about the demons, the ghosts, and the evil we encountered during our trip.

More importantly, I told him how I felt when I let God down, when I knew that what I was doing was not pleasing Him. Yet, here I was, a woman God still wanted to use to track and expel demons.

"I think it's because He knows your heart, Ains. God knows you love Him, and you will do whatever it takes to fulfill your purpose." He rose from the carpeted floor to leave. "Kyle told me once that he knew this life is only temporary. He knew who he was."

"What?" I asked, hoping he would impart some of Kyle's advice to me.

"A spiritual being in a temporary body. I don't think it mattered if Kyle was the Seer, the Protector, a Beacon, or whatever. He knew God thought of him as His son because of Jesus. Just like God thinks of us as His children too."

After Ben left my room, I laid on my floor thinking about Kyle's words to my little brother. I held up my hands and studied them. God gifted me with a temporary body, one I should take care of as a temple for the Holy Spirit. But God also gave me a soul, a spirit, that was set apart from this body. It was my spirit that communed with the Holy Spirit. It was my spirit that fought demons, not my temporary body. It was my spirit that Ben saw flickering under the body of my dying friend.

I sat up. It was my spirit that had to fight Jai-ish.

~ ~ ~

The look on Alec's face when I showed up at the police station unannounced was priceless. I'd thrown on a pair of jeans, black ankle boots, and my black puffer jacket over a tight sweater. I'd left my hair down with a face full of makeup so that I could bat my eyelashes at him.

The truth was, I hadn't been at the police station since I met Alec four years ago when he had me come in to review some video footage from the grocery store where I'd seen a demon, a Muladach, for the first time. Plus, today was the first morning that I had awakened and not fallen apart at the thought of Kyle.

Detective Wallace walked past me and placed a hand on my arm. "Miss Reynolds, I am so sorry about Kyle. He was a great guy. I really liked him."

I managed a smile. "Thank you, Detective. I know he liked you a lot."

"Ainsley?" Alec came around the corner.

"Hey, I brought you lunch." I held up the red and white carryout bag and a large cup of sweet tea from our favorite chicken place.

He took the bag from me and gave me a quick kiss.

Detective Wallace smiled. "I'll let you get to your lunch."

I followed Alec back to his desk. The metal desk was wider, and the surrounding walls were taller than I expected, more like a cubicle. I slid onto the corner of his desk. "This is nice. I thought the desks at the station would look like the ones on television; just a bunch of them shoved near each other in the middle of the floor. Why is it so clean in this area but grungy when you first walk in?"

Alec frowned. "As much as I love seeing you in the middle of the day, I doubt very much you made a trip here to bring me a grilled chicken sandwich."

"Of course not. I also brought you a fruit cup," I said, smiling as I took a sip of his too-sweet tea.

He eyeballed me for a second and then dug out the food and started eating as he read something on his computer screen. *Detective* Graham was no fun.

"Heard from Rafe yet?" I asked Alec.

He shook his head. "No. I stopped by his office this morning, and his secretary said he left for a business trip a few days ago."

"Do you think he is okay? I mean, do you think someone got to him the way they did Mark Tahl?"

Alec continued staring at the screen in front of him. "No unidentified body yet, so I don't think so."

When I didn't comment, he shifted his gaze over to me. "I'm sorry. That sounded insensitive. It's the nature of the job."

I nodded. "I know. I'm just wondering if Rafe is someone we can depend on or if he was-"

"Blowing smoke up our hind ends?" Alec finished my sentence for me.

"Yes, to put it so eloquently."

Alec sighed. "I don't know. I say we just continue without him. If he pops up, then great. I don't like not knowing either. I want to ride back down this weekend and see how Tilda and Stacia are getting along."

"This weekend? Do you want me to go with you?"

"You don't have to. Although I think Ben is dying to see Stacia again." Alec winked at me.

"The plan we worked out with Father Mahon and the others has me siphoning the Seer abilities from Finn and Robert *and* Ben. I should probably stay near him."

An officer stuck his head around Alec's cubicle. "Detective Graham, we have a situation."

Alec rose quickly and slid his arm around my waist while brushing his lips against my cheek. "Baby, I have to go," he whispered before leaving to follow the officer.

I quietly made my way through the hall as I listened to someone giving an urgent update to several officers and other men and women in a glass room. I leaned against the wall as I watched through the glass. I couldn't make out the words, only the alarming sound of a man's voice. Alec and Detective Wallace were both in the room, serious expressions on both their faces as they listened to the older bald man speaking from the podium. The man, who I was pretty sure was the Police Chief pointed to a flatscreen television behind him on the wall, but I couldn't see the images from where I stood. Instead, I watched Alec's face as he watched the screen.

His eyes widened, and then I was pretty sure I saw him say a curse word. From what I'd heard, he hadn't done that in a very long time. He pulled his cell phone out of his pocket and began scrolling. The bald man said something to him, but Alec held his index finger up, begging for one minute.

I shuddered when my phone rang in my back pocket. It continued ringing as I watched Alec turn his back to the glass wall, his tailored dress shirt straining against his back muscles. I pulled my cell from my pocket, read his name, and slid the green bar over.

"Alec?"

"Where are you?" he demanded. I watched as he turned back towards the flatscreen on the wall.

"I'm standing in the hall watching you."

Alec turned, and his eyes met mine. Less than a minute later, he was pulling me by my arm out the police station's front door while holstering his gun and pushing me into the back seat of his SUV, barking orders at Detective Wallace, who was running to keep up with him.

"Alec! What is it?" I yelled at him, but he continued climbing into the driver's seat as Wallace got into the passenger side. She'd barely clicked her seatbelt before he peeled out of the lot.

"Alec!" I yelled again as I slid across the backseat. "I can't get my seatbelt on. Slow down!"

"I can't slow down. Just get it on," he barked at me. He swerved again as he passed three cars getting on the interstate ramp, the siren blaring, and blue lights moving back and forth across the top of the windshield.

I finally managed to click the seatbelt in place as Alec swerved in and out of traffic. Detective Wallace was holding on to the bar in front of her for dear life.

"Graham, you're headed in the wrong direction."

"I know. We're getting Ainsley to safety."

"But that's not the proced-"

"I don't care about procedure, Wallace!" Alec yelled over the sirens.

"What did you see? What did you see on the screen?" I demanded.

Alec and Detective Wallace glanced at one another, but neither said a word. I decided I needed another tactic.

"Detective Wallace, please tell me what you saw on the screen. Please?"

Detective Wallace twisted her body around to see me better. "You can call me Anita." She gritted her teeth in a smile.

"Anita, what was on the television screen? What is so urgent?"

Anita opened her mouth to say something when Alec butted in. "Don't."

A single word with more commanding power than the Police Chief had had in all of his urgent meeting. It wasn't just the word. It was the way he said it. It was a mixture of force, danger, anger – and fear.

I swallowed as Alec's eyes met mine in the rearview mirror. Something was very, horribly wrong.

"Alec, turn the truck around. Take me to wherever he is."

"No."

"Alec, look at me."

His eyes glanced up at the rearview mirror again.

"It's Jai-ish, isn't it?"

He looked away. "Yes."

"Then take me to him."

"I can't lose you, Ainsley." He said the words without meeting my eyes in the mirror, his jaw set.

I touched his shoulder, felt the tension in the muscles. "I'm the only one left to face him, Alec. You have to take me there. This is my purpose."

This time his eyes shifted back to the mirror, eyes full of pain and misery. "He'll kill you, baby."

"Maybe." I forced my voice to rise above the siren's wailing and over the pounding of my heart. "But God already knows what's going to happen. He made me for such a time as this. Remember what you told me? All of this is bigger than us." I squeezed Alec's shoulder. "Please."

Alec silently took the next exit off the interstate, looped around, merged onto the highway, and headed back toward Locklyn.

# CHAPTER FIFTEEN

We arrived at an old, abandoned factory that I was pretty sure was once used to make nitroglycerin during World War II. The brick building was one level with strange peaks for the roof. My guess was the building was constructed that way to keep enemy pilots during the War from recognizing, and subsequently bombing, the plant. Police cars surrounded the building, and officers stood beside the cars with their weapons drawn.

After typing something into his phone, Alec got out of the truck and held up his ID for the officer closest to him. "Tell your superior that Ainsley Reynolds is here."

He opened the door and reached for my hand, but I withdrew.

"Tell me why we are here. You haven't told me anything. What is the situation?"

His jaw clenched, then he looked at the brick building, then back to me in the backseat. With a deep breath, he climbed into the back and slammed the door.

He looked at Anita. "Can you find the person in charge here? We'll be out in a minute."

She nodded, and with a glance at me, she was out of the truck, and it was just the two of us left in the SUV.

"This is a hostage situation. A boy was walking home from a friend's house a little bit ago, and someone grabbed him."

"But why am I here? Is there a demon involved? You said you believe it's Jai-ish." I struggled to make sense of this.

"The kidnapper asked for you specifically." He paused as if searching for the right words. "The boy taken is Ben."

I blinked. Surely, Alec was wrong. "I just saw Ben this morning. He was eating cereal at the kitchen counter."

"Then he went to Gavin's house, except Gavin wasn't home. He was walking back when someone grabbed him."

"Gavin practically lives next door," I said, my voice rising. "How could someone grab him that close to home?"

Alec put his hand over mine. "It doesn't matter how he did it. I texted Stephen a few minutes ago. Stephen and the others are on their way. And yes, I think that is Jai-ish up there with Ben. The kidnapper said that he has a bomb, so no one is to enter the building but you."

"And, you were what? Going to take me to safety and away from my brother, who is in danger? Just let Jai-ish kill Ben?" I punched Alec's arm as hard as I could.

His eyes twitched, but he didn't move. "I reacted. But you were right. You are the only one who might be able to stop this. Jai-ish is not going to let Ben live either way."

I blinked again. "I dislike your Detective Graham voice. It sounds heartless."

It was the only thing I could think of to say. I stared at the brick building through the windshield. If I had to enter the building alone because of a bomb, then I would need to channel Finn's and Robert's powers from a distance. There was a chance I could channel Ben's power once inside.

Maybe that would be enough.

"Okay," I whispered.

Alec only hesitated a second before opening the door and helping me out. He must have decided that my snide comment about his heartless professional voice and me physically assaulting him wasn't worth a fight moments before I walked into a trap.

A man ran up and introduced himself to us. In a whirlwind, suddenly, my jacket was off, and my sweater pulled up as the man – whose name I hadn't paid attention to – was attaching a wire to my bare skin and popping a small bud into my ear. He had me say the word *testing* and then announced to Alec and another man standing nearby that I was ready.

Was I ready?

The man who had stood by silently moved to action as he and Alec began rushing me toward the building.

"Miss Reynolds, when you speak to the kidnapper, I need you to remain calm. Do not provoke him. We don't know what he wants. If he wants something that we can give him, tell him that you will talk to us. Ask him if you can call Detective Graham or me and ask the police for what he wants."

I watched the man's mouth as it moved, then slowly raised my gaze to Alec's. He was aware of the real game at play here. Whoever Jai-ish possessed didn't give two hoots about worldly things like money or a helicopter. Jai-ish wanted to kill my body, and probably Ben's before I had a chance to banish him from the Earth.

"Do you understand, Miss Reynolds?" the man repeated.

"Yes. I know what I have to do."

Alec's face was unreadable, but I could guess what he was thinking – I was the only one who could stop Jai-ish, and yet, the chances of me surviving another attack were slim. I gave him a slight smile, then turned toward the building.

His voice came through the pod tucked neatly in my ear, "I love you, Ainsley."

With one last look at him over my shoulder, I opened the metal door to the old factory and stepped inside. "I love you more, Alec."

~   ~   ~

It took a moment for my eyes to adjust inside the dark building. The smell of mold and dampness hit my nostrils. In the parking lot, someone had shoved a flashlight into my hands, and I flicked it on.

I closed my eyes and prayed. *God, please help me banish Jai-ish. Please let Ben be safe; let him stay safe. If there is an archangel you can spare, can you please send them my way? I could use the help.*

I kept my eyes closed as I controlled my breathing and forced my heart rate to slow. I quieted my mind as I listened for what Kyle referred to as 'the sound under the silence.' I did not feel any vibrations from a Muladach. Then again, Jai-ish was much harder to detect since he could hide inside of a human.

"Robert and Finn are here," came Alec's voice through the tiny earbud.

I pictured Robert in my mind with his dark curls. I pictured the light, the soul light, that Ben could see. I then imagined that I could reach out and touch Robert's light, pulling a little bit for myself. Next, I pictured Finn and his light, stretching a bit more of it into me.

When I opened my eyes, I felt stronger and more attuned to the atmosphere around me.

"Where are you, Ben?" I whispered.

A thudding sound on the other side of the wall shook the dust and peeling paint loose. As the particles dropped in front of me, I began the search for my brother. The factory was disorienting at best. The rooms in the building connected through individual metal doors, giving off the sensation of a complete building within itself. It was as if I was on board a train, moving from car to car, except these were large warehouse-type rooms that seemed to stretch out forever.

When I reached the fourth such area, I heard the thudding again as I opened a metal door that led to an open space. It looked like the manufacturing company had demolished all the individual offices that had once stood in this portion of the building and only left behind the concrete floor, metal pillars, and cracked windows. In the middle of the space was my little brother tied to a metal chair, duct tape over his mouth. I forced my breathing to remain controlled. Ben couldn't help with his mouth taped.

Ben and I stared at each other, and then he looked swiftly to his right. I followed the movement to see a man leaning against the wall near a window. He wisely stood not too close to the glass in case of snipers.

"Good. You came," the man said as he looked me up and down. "I thought I was going to have to blow up this building without you." Thomas, Mark Tahl's assistant, sporting a black eye, turned his busted lips up into a demonic grin.

He walked closer to Ben but stopped when he saw me start towards them. "Slow down, Ainsley Grace Reynolds. I'm not quite ready to kill you yet. This time around."

Thomas reached out to pat Ben on the head, but I tuned him out and closed my eyes. I continued to see Ben in my mind as I pulled his light from his body. In my imagination, Ben's light was so much brighter than Finn's or Robert's.

When I opened my eyes, Jai-ish was watching me curiously while Ben was struggling to catch his breath. Had I done that? Or did Jai-ish do something to him while my eyes were closed?

"Let him go, Jai-ish."

"Why should I? Because he can't breathe?"

"Take the tape off his mouth."

Jai-ish shook his head. "No, Beacons are better off with their mouths shut. They only hurl insults and banishments at me. As a matter of fact, since you are the first female Beacon, I have something special planned for you." He walked behind Ben and placed his hands on Ben's shoulders. "I'm going to take my time and sew your mouth shut. You'll be alive, but you won't be able to cause much trouble until I see fit to kill you. Perhaps I will sew both your mouths shut."

The tremor of fear I felt before moved through me, and I pushed it, and the bile coming up my throat, as far down as I could. "You can do this before your bomb detonates?"

A smile crept across Jai-ish's face, or rather the face of the man he possessed. Thomas had been handsome once with his blonde hair and beard, big muscles on a shorter body of probably five foot nine. Even now, he wore jeans, a green military jacket, and a brown beanie on his head.

"No bomb, I lied. Look at you, Ainsley. Even in the face of death, you are checking me out. Have you no shame?"

"You used Thomas to kill Mark Tahl, didn't you?"

Jai-ish threw his head back and laughed. "Yes, but the boy was a horrible shot, wasn't he? He was supposed to aim for the man's chest, not blow his head apart. He could have easily hit you and the boy Drekr." He rested his elbows on Ben's shoulders and smiled. "Speaking of Drekr. I did not expect him to sacrifice his life for you. Perhaps now you will love him as much as he loved you." He cocked his head. "When it came to you, he was a hopeless romantic, but you couldn't see it. Nothing worse than unrequited love. Although he would have taken you up on a physical relationship – if you'd only asked." His mouth turned up into a snarl.

A pang hit my heart. He wanted me to feel guilt. "How did you get that black eye and busted lip?"

Jai-ish slapped the back of Ben's head. "This little wanna-be Seer. As if Yahweh would really use him. I must admit, strong thing to be so young. It really is a pity that I'm going to have to rip him apart."

I raised my hand, pointing at the man. "I banish you, Jai-ish, from this realm in the name of Jesus Christ. You have no power here." I felt the warm sensation of the others' powers moving through me.

Jai-ish took a step backward, away from Ben. Just a little more. I pushed the light I had collected outward.

"Jai-ish, I call on you. You are bound and banished from this realm."

Jai-ish growled at me as he took another step back, then waved his hand. For a second, I was blinded by an image of Kyle laughing at something I had once said during a picnic with my family, the sunlight making his blue eyes almost clear.

"Oh no, you don't," I growled back as I pushed the image away. I moved more of the Seers' light through me. "Begone, demon!"

Jai-ish hit me with yet another image, one a lot more graphic than the first. Before I could push it away, he waved his arm, and my legs flew out from underneath me as my body hurled backward into one of the metal pillars. I bounced from the beam onto the floor, my face scraping the cold concrete.

I could hear Jai-ish laughing. I needed to get up and face him before he descended on me. Except I couldn't move. My mind was blank. There were no images. Why couldn't I move?

"It's your spinal cord," Jai-ish said from somewhere above me. He crouched and slid his hands over my arms as he pushed me onto my back. "I think I may have broken your body. At least, your spine."

*God, no. Please, no.*

He gently moved my hair away from my face so that I could see him clearly. "Your human bodies are so fragile. Decaying almost from the moment of birth." He leaned down close to my ear and whispered, "I think it's a design flaw."

"Ainsley? What's happening?" Alec's voice came through the earbud.

I could hear Ben whimpering from across the room.

Just then, there was what sounded like an explosion of glass and a brilliant, bright light. I tried to turn my head, but I couldn't. My eyes followed Jai-ish as he stood, regarding something in the room with us.

"Raphael, so good of you to join us. I heard you were helping the Beacon and Malus Navis. Where have you been, Brother? You look weary."

"I have not been your brother for a long time, Jai-ish. Did you truly believe that your minions could stop me? Michael, the great archangel, is finishing them off as I speak. It's time that you go back to Hell for a while, Jai-ish." It was Rafe's voice, but it sounded thunderous in the room. The phrase *entertaining angels unaware* flitted through my mind.

"Unless you want to fight me for three days, then it is not worth it. I broke your Beacon." Jai-ish looked down at me, a smirk playing on his lips.

"She is not broken, Jai-ish. I can see her spirit from here; it is on fire. She can set it free. She is also not the only Beacon whose powers are in this room."

Jai-ish jerked his head up as I heard the ripping sound of duct tape. Then Rafe's voice, "Now, Benjamin!"

I heard Ben, first unsure of himself, and then stronger as he recited the words I had used on Jai-ish. The man possessed by the demon moved against the wall, snarling and screaming, cursing at Rafe and Ben, at me, and at God.

I knew what I had to do, and although I was terrified, I remembered my father's words from his journal. I needed to push past the fear. I wasn't the Seer meant to banish Jai-ish. But I was the Seer strong enough to funnel all of our abilities into my brother. With my final breath, I let go.

My soul moved away from the heap that was my body and floated over it, taking in the brightness emanating from Rafe and Ben. In my hands, I held a pulsating ball of light; my power, Robert's and Finn's powers. Instinctively, I knew to throw the light to Ben. I watched as the fireball landed in his chest, and Ben's voice suddenly grew louder and almost as thunderous as Rafe's voice.

Jai-ish was against the wall, snarling and cursing us. A blinding figure dressed in battle armor held him firmly in place. With a crack, Jai-ish hit Rafe with such force that the archangel stumbled backward. Jai-ish slid back down to the floor, landing with a supernatural thud that shook the building.

"You should have come better prepared, Raphael."

Jai-ish threw a right hook and a bright light flew out from him, headed straight for a restrained Ben. Not sure if it would work, I flew over in front of Ben and allowed the light to hit me. My spirit flickered for a moment, but it held.

Jai-ish narrowed his eyes at me. "Beacons. Trouble when they are alive and trouble when they are dead."

As he raised his arm again to attack us, Rafe moved like lightening, catching Jai-ish by the throat as he thrust the man/demon into the ceiling and then slammed him into the concrete floor. The earth quaked below us and Ben screamed.

"Say the words again, Ben!" I yelled, hoping my brother could hear me.

Ben immediately began reciting the words in a loud voice as Rafe pinned Jai-ish against the wall again. Rafe's gold armor glinted in the light, blinding me for a moment.

Then with a sizzling sound, the man possessed by Jai-ish burst into a mist of blood. The dark form of Jai-ish remained for only a moment before it, too, disappeared. Immediately, my soul was sucked back into my body. Ben yelped, and I tried to cry out to him, but my lips refused to move.

Alec was screaming at me through the earpiece. I'd forgotten that the police squad below could hear everything.

Rafe moved into my field of vision, but it wasn't Rafe. He appeared similar, but his countenance was so bright I could barely make out his features. He leaned down close to my face. At the same time, I heard Ben above my head, crying.

"Miss Reynolds, Jai-ish has hurt your body dreadfully. However, he did not have permission from God to kill or maim you. I'm going to run my hands over you. You will feel a warm sensation, and it will hurt as the nerves reconnect and activate again. You will be in a great deal of pain, and for that, I am truly sorry."

Rafe closed his eyes and ran his hands over my face, down my neck, chest, abs, and each one of my legs. Next, he moved his hands under my body from the top of my head to my feet. I watched him, and when he opened his sapphire blue eyes, he kissed me lightly on the forehead, and an excruciating pain hit me. I moaned, then screamed as I managed to turn onto my side. I could not move without being in utter misery.

Alec's voice blasted in my ear again, but Rafe very calmly removed the earpiece and handed it to Ben. "Thank you, Benjamin Gerald Reynolds. Your ability as the Beacon and the magnified powers from the others allowed me to expel Jai-ish in moments instead of days! You and your sister are very special. Take care of one another. Perhaps I will meet you again."

Rafe stood and walked out of my field of vision before I passed out from the pain.

# EPILOGUE

The sun peaked out from behind the trees behind my mother's house one morning a week later. One week after everything had changed. At least four inches of snow packed onto our lawn, with more falling heavily. Standing at the patio doors, nestled in a plush pink robe, I watched the snowflakes falling so fast that I couldn't make them out. Instead, they appeared as fast-moving tears escaping from heaven. I hardened my grip on my coffee mug until my fingers threatened to make an indent in the stoneware.

To my left, was a new table set against the wall with framed pictures of our family with Kyle. Pictures from our excursions to Los Angeles, Texas, Florida. Pictures from a family picnic and a beach trip. We'd even framed several selfies that Kyle had insisted he and I take together – the ones he promptly posted on his social media every time with the caption "my little sis" which always caused a rash of questions from his fans. I swallowed the growing lump in my throat.

"I thought you would sleep later," Alec's voice came from the kitchen. He had spent every night in the family room to be close to us since my release from the hospital and my miraculous recovery. I poked my head around the wall to see him standing in pajama bottoms and a tee shirt making himself a cup of coffee.

"It's cold outside, and the snow is falling," I answered, turning back to the door.

A moment later, Alec joined me and wrapped his free arm around my shoulders. "Are you okay?" he whispered.

I leaned my head against his shoulder. "I am. So much has happened that I'm still trying to decompress. Ben seems to be taking everything in stride."

After the initial shock of what happened, Ben quizzed Father Mahon, Finn, and Robert on everything about Seers and Protectors. His strength and tenacity reminded me of Dad which had me worried about his future.

"Come downstairs," Alec said before kissing me on the cheek and moving away.

I carefully and quietly carried my cup through the living room where Stephen slept soundly on the pull-out couch and down the stairs to the family room. Alec had already put the sofa bed back into its original position in the sectional. I pushed away the memories of Kyle's last days in this room.

"Are you sleeping okay down here?"

"I am, once I got past Stephen's snoring upstairs. I'd forgotten how loud he is."

We both smiled, remembering our time at the hotel in South Carolina and Alec rooming with Stephen for a while. Alec sat down on the sectional on the far end. "Come here," he said, motioning me with the crook of his index finger.

I curled up next to him, carefully moving my coffee mug away and situating myself, as he pulled the recliner section for us to stretch out. My back was severely bruised, but I was thankful I could move. Alec took the mug away from me and set it next to his on the end table. He wrapped his arm around me.

"Careful, Detective. Taking a woman's first cup of coffee away in the morning is a murderous crime in this town."

Alec smiled, then reached into the pocket of his pajamas and pulled out a small blue box.

My heart stopped beating, and I had to remind myself that now was not the time for a cardiac arrest. I looked up into Alec's green eyes.

He played with the box in his hand for a moment, searching for the right words. "Ainsley, you have driven me crazy more times than I can count, sent me on jealous rages, and tore my heart out by ignoring me. You have made me see supernatural things that I never thought existed. You made me fall in love with you by showing up unannounced at my door wearing a plaid shirt with a loose button."

He pulled me closer to him. "All that being said, I love you more than anyone else on this planet. I want to spend the rest of my life with you. I want to have oodles of children with you to fill that estate up in South Carolina. I want to look across a room and know that no matter what the insurmountable odds look like, you and I will still have each other in the end."

He moved off the sectional until he was kneeling in front of me. I didn't mind that the moment had come, and I still wore my pajamas and plushest robe, my blonde hair wrapped up in a high bun, and not wearing a stitch of makeup. The moment was perfect.

"Ainsley Grace Reynolds, will you do me the honor of marrying me and becoming Mrs. Graham?" Alec opened the box. It held a sparkling white gold ring with a white princess-cut diamond surrounded by rows of blue diamonds.

"Yes," I whispered, tears streaming down my face, despite my wish for them to stop. "Yes, I will marry you!" I hugged Alec and kissed him. Then pulled away quickly to add, "But we have to have the wedding after I graduate college in the Spring. That way, we can move to South Carolina, if you want to live there, and I can teach and work on my Master's degree there, and-"

Alec kissed me again.

**THE END**

# A LETTER FROM THE AUTHOR

**Dear Reader,**

Thank you for coming along on these adventures with new Christians, Ainsley and Alec. The truth is…being a Christian is hard and spiritual warfare is real. Maybe you aren't expelling demons like the Muladach or Jai-ish back to Hell. But don't be fooled. If you are a committed Christian working to enlarge His kingdom, there is a demonic assignment placed on you daily.

Maybe take some cues from Ainsley. I know I have in the last few years. Surround yourself with other believers, remove toxic influences from your life, steep yourself in God's word, and PRAY. You might want to always keep prayer in the forefront.

The Beacon was supposed to be the last book in The Muladach Series. However, after receiving numerous emails and messages from readers, there will be at least a novella and two more books. The novella is entitled The Seer and is about Gerald Reynolds, Ainsley's father, two years before his death. The next book is about a twenty-something Ben as he navigates life while serving as a Seer.

Ainsley, Alec, and the others will also make appearances. Both books will be available in 2022.

The last book I am currently outlining in the series includes the adventures of Ainsley and Kyle before Alec came back into the picture. I know, I miss Kyle too.

To sum up, there will be more in The Muladach Series! Take these flawed characters seriously, as I hope I have made them as life-like as possible. No one is perfect, but God doesn't choose the perfect. He chooses the flawed, the broken, the betrayed, and the contrite, and He makes us perfect in His eyes through the grace of Jesus Christ.

Feel free to reach out to me with prayer requests or just to say hello at:

**authormelissaplantz@fireandgracepublishing.com**

Oh, and remember to leave a review on Amazon, Goodreads, and Bookbub if you love the books! You wouldn't believe how much this helps indie authors and publishers get the word out about the books.

Love in Christ,

Melissa Plantz

# ABOUT THE AUTHOR

**M**elissa Plantz is an author, Christian, and the founder of Fire and Grace Publishing. As the author of the spiritual warfare devotional series, *Take the Realm*, and of two Christian novels (*Fire and Grace*, *The Muladach*), Melissa is dedicated to equipping today's Christians with the tools for spiritual warfare through the power of storytelling. She believes that it's never been more important to spread the message of Christ, and that maintaining faith in the modern world is a powerful key to fulfillment and happiness.

When not writing, she enjoys spending time with her husband, children, and grandchildren. She currently lives in West Virginia, but she dreams of moving permanently to a beach off the coast of North Carolina. Connect with her at AuthorMelissaPlantz@fireandgracepublishing.com

For more information visit:

**fireandgracepublishing.com**

# ALSO BY MELISSA PLANTZ

## AND FIRE AND GRACE PUBLISHING

Take the Realm: 10 Days of Spiritual Battle Plans to Reignite the Weary Warrior

*Fire and Grace*


**THE MULADACH SERIES**

The Muladach

The Maddening

The Beacon

Keep your eyes out for The Seer, releasing as a novella in 2022!